FABER has published children's books since 1929. T. S. Eliot's *Old Possum's Book of Practical Cats* and Ted Hughes' *The Iron Man* were amongst the first. Our catalogue at the time said that 'it is by reading such books that children learn the difference between the shoddy and the genuine'. We still believe in the power of reading to transform children's lives. All our books are chosen with the express intention of growing a love of reading, a thirst for knowledge and to cultivate empathy. We pride ourselves on responsible editing. Last but not least, we believe in kind and inclusive books in which all children feel represented and important.

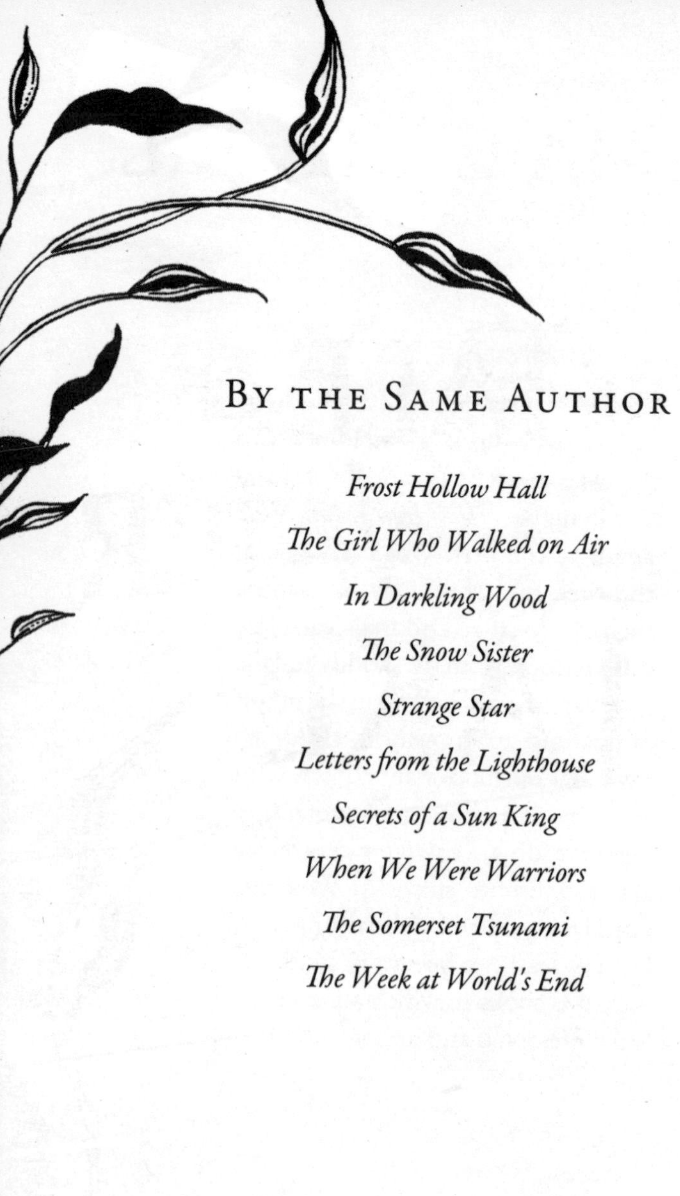

By the Same Author

Frost Hollow Hall

The Girl Who Walked on Air

In Darkling Wood

The Snow Sister

Strange Star

Letters from the Lighthouse

Secrets of a Sun King

When We Were Warriors

The Somerset Tsunami

The Week at World's End

EMMA CARROLL

THE TALE OF TRUTHWATER LAKE

First published in 2022
by Faber & Faber Limited
Bloomsbury House,
74–77 Great Russell Street,
London WC1B 3DA
faber.co.uk
This paperback edition first published 2023

Typeset in Garamond Premier by Typo•glyphix, Burton-on-Trent DE14 3HE
Printed by CPI Group (UK) Ltd, Croydon CR0 4YY

A CIP record for this book
is available from the British Library

ISBN 978–0–571–33286–1

Printed and bound in the UK on FSC paper in line with our continuing commitment to ethical business practices, sustainability and the environment.
For further information see faber.co.uk/environmental-policy

2 4 6 8 10 9 7 5 3 1

For Becky and Chrissy,
my curry-night queens

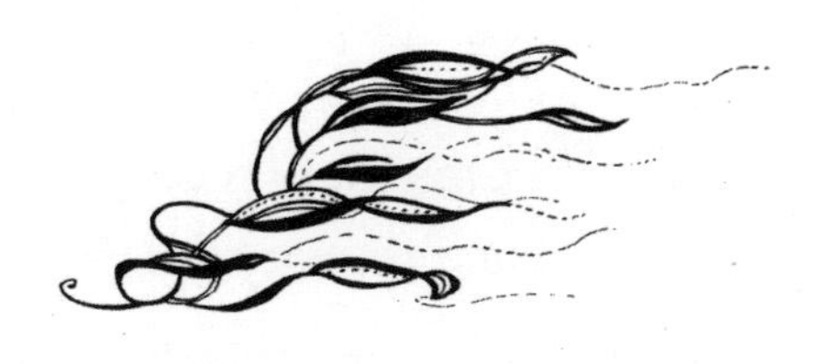

1.
SUMMER, 2032
POLLY

Late one night when it's too hot to sleep, I catch my brother climbing over our balcony. He's about to lower himself on to the neighbour's wheelie bin when he sees me watching.

'Go back to bed, Polly!' Joel hisses.

'No chance.' I've spotted the towel under his arm, the bag on his shoulder, a dead giveaway that he's going to the beach.

'You can't come,' he protests. 'You can't even swim.'

'I did fifty metres at the pool today, *actually*,' I say though I don't mention how tough it was.

Joel sighs. 'Okay! Come! Just . . . you know . . . be *quiet*?'

I mime zipping my mouth shut. Though Joel and I are unmistakably related – curly dark hair, Dad's green eyes and Mum's bumpy nose – I'm very much the chatty one, it's true. Also, it's the middle of the night, and my device shows the temperature's twenty-five degrees, so it's way too hot to argue.

The heatwave started just before we broke up for the summer, the last days of term spent melting in classrooms as hot as griddles. It's five weeks into the holidays now, and we've spent most of it stuck inside our tiny flat. The government brought in an emergency law that says when the temperature is over forty-two we have to stay indoors.

'*Another* ruddy lockdown!' was how Dad reacted to the news.

When I was a baby, there'd been a killer virus that meant no one could go out for months. Back then we didn't even have a garden – and still don't – which makes the fact my parents run an actual gardening business sort of weird.

Yet we *do* live across the road from the sea – the English Channel, to be exact. In winter, when there's a storm, the waves crash against our windows and the sea floods our street, all foamy brown and briny. And it rains and rains and rains – sometimes for days on end, sometimes all at once in a downpour – and eventually the drains bubble and the city floods too. It's why Mum insisted I learn how to swim.

'Don't roll your eyes, Pol,' she'd chided. 'If you got stuck in a flood one day, it could save your life.'

Which might be true, though so is Mum's knack for spotting every potential catastrophe.

This summer, it's the heatwave that's done the damage, burning shoulders, scorching lawns, melting pavements. People say the weather never used to be like this. It's on the news constantly: droughts in Sudan, rising sea levels in the Bahamas, footage of flooded homes and starving people and animals. There's no denying we've made a mess of our planet.

Still, it's nice to see my brother smiling for once, his teeth glinting in the dark.

'I s'pose you can raise the alarm if I drown,' Joel admits. 'Though realistically, you're the one more likely to—'

'All right,' I interrupt. 'You're the better swimmer. Point made.'

He's also a better cook, better at schoolwork, better at everything. I'm the average one in our family.

The beach is steep, shingle, on the other side of a main, well-lit road. We reach it down some steps. The shush of the sea, in and out, is restful, like sleep breathing, and at the water's edge I let the tide lap my toes. On the horizon, the red lights of the wind turbines wink, and I wonder if anyone has ever swum out to them.

'You know it's illegal to swim the English Channel if you're under sixteen?' I say, remembering a random fact from earlier when I was online, avoiding homework.

Our teacher set us this task to ask an elderly person about their life – proud moments and regrets, that sort of stuff. I don't know any old people, only Miss Gee, who's just moved in downstairs, and she's not very friendly.

Joel kicks the shingle. 'No Channel swimming for us tonight, then?'

'Nope. The first person to swim the English Channel was Captain Matthew Webb in 1875. Bet you didn't know that.'

'I didn't.'

'And,' I choose a flat pebble, skim it across the water, 'it took him nearly *twenty-two* hours! That's almost a *whole* day – like three mealtimes and a night's sleep, and a day at school. Imagine being in the sea all that time!'

'Hmmm.'

It's the idea of anyone swimming so far that I can't get my head round, especially when I struggle to do a length at the pool. All that water underneath you, not knowing what's down there lurking; the very idea makes me shudder. I imagine, just as Mum would, tomorrow's tragic *Evening Argus* headline:

LOCAL GIRL POLLY CARRAWAY, 12,
LOST IN CHANNEL SWIM ACCIDENT

I back away from the water's edge.

'You know what?' I decide. 'Someone should stay here and guard our stuff. You go on in.'

Joel reads me instantly. 'Thought you were getting better at swimming.'

'I am. Sort of.'

'We're not swimming to France. You'll be all right.'

Joel sets off in the direction of the old pier. I follow, with a niggling feeling that this is where he wants to swim. Years ago, before I was born, most of the pier burned down, and what's left sits a few metres offshore like a giant iron cage. I'd prefer somewhere more open, without the seaweed or bars of rusting metal looming over us. And I certainly don't want to go in by myself.

'Wait for me!' I cry, hurrying to catch up.

Joel strolls on, oblivious, hands in pockets, shoulders hunched under his too-big T-shirt. He's been miles away all summer, my brother, lost inside his head. Mum says he's being a typical teenager, but I can't help thinking there's more to it somehow. When we're level with the old pier, Joel stops and takes off his T-shirt, steps out of his jeans. He's got trunks on underneath. 'You coming?'

I hesitate.

'C'mon, Pol,' he coaxes. 'You said you swam fifty metres.'

I tighten my ponytail. Fifty metres in a pool isn't the same as in the sea, in the dark, and anyway, it wasn't *exactly* fifty metres, and I did stop when the water went up my nose. Sasha, who's meant to be my friend, laughed so much the lifeguard told her off. I didn't find it funny, but the rest of our swimming class did. Ten people all laughing at me.

'You know I'm no good at this,' I said to her afterwards. 'And you making fun of me in front of everyone really didn't help.'

'I'm sorry, okay?' she said, but I could still see the laughter in her face. I told her so too.

That was when she flipped.

'It's not all about you, Polly!'

We haven't spoken since.

It's imagining Sasha's reaction when I tell her I've swum around the pier that persuades me in the end.

'Just don't swim off and leave me,' I warn my brother. 'Or pretend to be a shark.'

Joel gives me an 'as if I would' look.

I slip off my sandals. I didn't get the chance to change into my costume, so I go in wearing my pyjamas. The thin cotton puffs up, all air, but once my shoulders are under and I start to swim, I realise Joel is right: I can do this. He's just ahead of me, his arm a white flash as it breaks the water. Together, we aim for the outline of the pier. I try not to think about the water getting deeper beneath us or that if I put my feet down now there'll be nothing to stand on.

Instead, I focus on the horizon: it's what a Channel swimmer does, so the internet told me, eyes and brain always on what's up ahead. My arms move slowly; my body feels awkward in the water. Though I splash and kick, I'm barely moving, but at least I'm not drowning. I do my best not to wonder how far down the seabed is, or notice the pier's legs giving off a slimy glimmer in the darkness. A few more strokes and we're almost level with the furthest point of the pier. I'm actually *enjoying* how cool the sea feels. We've all been so hot, so bad-tempered for weeks, but this is just delicious.

'All right, Polly Rogers?' Joel calls. It's his stupid nickname for me. 'Want to keep going?'

'Maybe, I'll—'

There's a flash above us.

'Geez!' Joel cries.

My first thought is it's lightning. A cold, sickly panic creeps up from my feet. Now my arms don't want to work properly, and I can't find a way to keep my chin above the water. The flash comes again, just above us on the pier. It's a camera flash, I realise, from someone's device. There are voices, laughter, the creak and ting of someone clambering across the metalwork.

'Might have guessed,' Joel mutters.

Something tells me he knows who's up there. I swallow water, start coughing. Joel swoops towards me, tipping me backwards, crooking a hand under my jaw. We lurch about, a tangle of bumping elbows and too many legs.

'Thought you could swim,' Joel hisses.

I can't speak. Can't breathe.

The camera flashes again. And again.

I'm drowning, I think, and someone's taking pictures. My arms and legs are too heavy to move, yet Joel finds the right stroke to swim us away from the pier.

'It's all right, I've got you,' my brother murmurs.

Somehow he gets us back to the beach. When I see the street lights, the cars parked along the seafront road, for one bewildering second I think we've made it to France. Then I feel the shingle beneath my feet. My legs are so wobbly I have to crawl up the beach on my hands and knees, coughing up a whole ocean of water.

Joel stands for a moment, stunned.

'I'm fine, thanks for asking,' I mutter. I'm never going

swimming again, not ever. No matter how hot I get or how long this heatwave lasts.

Joel reaches for his clothes.

'Don't you dare tell anyone what's just happened,' he says, trembling so much it scares me.

'I won't,' I say.

We'll both be in mega trouble if our parents find out where we've been. But when I look at Joel properly, it's not me he's staring at, it's the pier again.

'Who was it up there?' I ask.

Joel bites his lip. 'No one.'

He's lying. I heard them laughing. *And* they were taking photos of us.

*

It's worse than photos. The next morning there's a murky film clip posted online of me thrashing about in the sea, and Joel struggling to keep me from sinking. I feel sick, and guilty at all the comments under the post, all the likes. It's my fault this has happened. My fault for following him down to the beach when all he wanted was a quiet swim by himself.

'I *am* sorry,' I try to tell him. I feel terrible. This is far worse than falling out with Sasha.

Normally Joel doesn't get angry, but this has really bothered him, and he bats away my apology.

'Save it, Pol. I'm never going anywhere with you again, so don't ask,' he replies.

True to his word, Joel keeps his promise for the next couple of days, and I keep mine. I don't tell a soul what happened on the beach that night: well, only you.

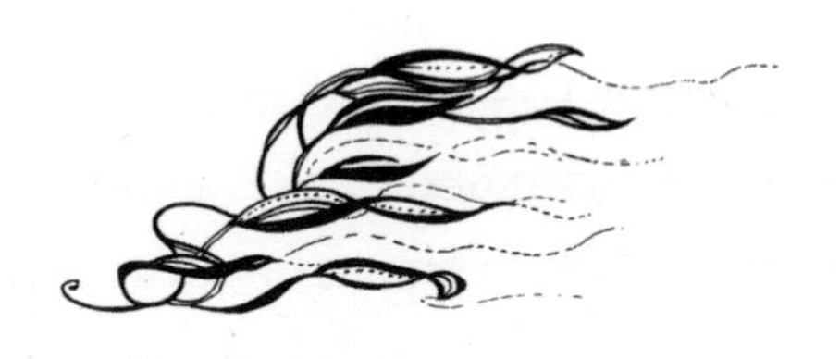

2.
SUMMER, 2032
POLLY

Soon enough Mum notices something's not right.

'You're quiet, Pol,' she says, studying me across the breakfast table. 'You okay?'

I flop dramatically over my cereal bowl.

'It's too hot,' I reply, which is the answer for everything these days. 'And . . . I'm worried—' I stop before mentioning Joel, who, since the swimming clip, has been glued to his device. Still, Mum pounces on what I've said.

'Worried about what? Going back to school?' She asks because Joel was bullied at school last term, though they never got to the bottom of who was doing it. I can't imagine this film clip will help.

'I've got some tricky homework to do,' I admit. 'But no, it's not school.'

'Sasha, then? You've hardly seen her this holidays. Have you two fallen out?'

Reluctantly, I sit up. 'She was mean to me at swimming.'

'How?'

'She joked about me. Said I swam like a poodle.'

'Oh.' Mum leans back in her seat. She gets that 'poodle' is a reference to my ridiculously curly hair. She knows how I wish I had straight, well-behaved hair like hers.

'The whole class laughed,' I add weakly.

It sounds childish now but I'd tried really hard to swim those fifty metres, so what Sasha said did hurt.

'And it's . . . it's *this*.' I gesture at our tiny kitchen. 'Being stuck inside all summer. I'm sick of it.'

Then there's Mum and Dad, super stressed about keeping their gardening business going in temperatures hotter than the Sahara. And Joel, who stays in his bedroom with the door shut. We don't dare play our music loudly, or make too much noise, because our new downstairs neighbour bangs on her ceiling if we do. She calls our family 'the Clydesdales', whatever that means, and says we sound as if we've got cement in our shoes.

I take a spoonful of now soggy cereal.

'Wish we could go to Jessie's,' I say, thinking wistfully about our favourite aunt.

In past summer holidays when the gardening business was booming, Joel and I were often packed off to stay with her so our parents could work. Jessie lives in an eco-house she built herself. It's small and basic – bad internet, compost toilets – but the garden is huge and overlooks a reservoir. It's all trees and water in every direction. Better still, she works long hours as a community nurse, so we basically look after ourselves.

Mum sighs. 'Jessie *did* mention inviting you, love, but she thought you'd both get bored.'

'I wouldn't,' I insist, though I daren't speak for Joel.

'Hmmm.' Mum considers it. 'Maybe we could sort something out, then. *If* we can find cheap fuel to get you there.'

I cross my fingers, double tight, on both hands, for what could be the best news in weeks.

*

Immediately, Mum sets off in a whirlwind of chivvying us, phoning Jessie, checking fuel prices.

'I'm already packed,' Joel calls from his bedroom.

I'd worried he wouldn't want to go to Jessie's and be responsible for his annoying little sister. But as he's not normally this super organised, I take it as a sign he does want to come, which is a relief.

Once I've done my own packing – and even though I'm too excited to concentrate – I get out that piece of homework I'm stuck on. I join Dad at the kitchen table, where he's researching drought-resistant garden plants.

'Am I *really* the oldest person you know?' he laughs when I ask him to help.

Mum's parents are on a walking holiday in Scotland, and Dad's died when he was a teenager. So yes, at this precise moment, he is.

'Sorry, Dad,' I say, pen poised. 'Tell me something you were proud of in your life, please.'

He looks at the ceiling, thinking.

'Tomatoes,' he says. 'I used to grow some real beauties from seed.'

I don't write this down.

'What about regrets?' I try instead.

'Tomatoes,' he says again. 'I wish I'd space for a polytunnel. Nothing beats the taste of a home-grown tomato.'

I give up. He's not taking this seriously. The homework will have to wait.

Yet by nightfall our old hybrid van is part charged,

part full of fuel, and everything's arranged. We *are* going to Jessie's, which I suppose proves I'm not completely useless.

*

The next morning we're all up super early to beat the heat. Though it's not yet seven o'clock, the sky is a pale, simmering blue, the warmth building. Outside on the rooftops, the seagulls screech half-heartedly, already too hot to care. With room for only three passengers in our van, it's Mum who is driving us to Exmoor. Jessie is, after all, her sister, and Dad, for the first time in ages, has a day's work on the communal gardens in the middle of our square.

Down in the street, he's taking what equipment he needs out of the van. The pavement is littered with rakes, shears, hoes, hedge trimmers, and through the open kitchen window Dad's good-mood whistling drifts up, as does his voice saying 'Sorry, mate' each time a passer-by has to step over the tools.

I'm in a good mood too. Even Joel, headphones on, slurping his breakfast, is tapping his feet to his music. He's been as excited as me about going away, so I'm hoping I'm just about forgiven. His device has still been going off day and night with notifications about the clip. It's going to be such a relief to get to Jessie's, with its bad internet, and no signal for miles.

Mum joins us in the kitchen and pours herself some muesli. She's fresh from the shower, her hair still wrapped in a towel. There's a national bread shortage currently because the wheat harvest was poor. It means we can't have toast, which is another reason why this summer has been so rubbish.

'Aren't you hungry?' I ask, noticing the tiny amount in Mum's bowl.

'Oh, Polly, not with your mouth full, please,' she groans.

She clutches her stomach suddenly and rushes off to the bathroom. Personally, I don't think chewed-up cereal looks that terrible, but I'm pretty sure my mum's just been sick.

*

Mum ends up back in bed. It's really not like her to be ill.

'Is she all right?' I ask Dad.

'It's just the heat,' Dad says, looking anxious enough for both of us. This isn't like him, either. Of my parents, he's the optimistic one, so his sudden seriousness is worrying. I guess it goes without saying the trip to Jessie's is off.

But no.

Apparently, we're catching the train instead. At the station, Dad comes in with us to buy our tickets on a credit card he rarely uses. The place is heaving with people in vest tops and sundresses, sweaty-faced, sweaty-haired, the smell of sunscreen everywhere. Our train is already boarding. It's a rush to say goodbye.

'Keep us posted on how Mum's doing,' I plead.

'Course. I'll let Jessie know the change of plan,' Dad promises as we give him a last hug.

Inside, the train is packed. There aren't any spare seats, so we stand in the aisle for the next few stops. Joel starts listening to music. I stare out of the window, glad of the change of scenery, though everywhere looks depressingly hot. We pass a park where the grass is bleached white, and the swings hang empty because no one takes their kids out in the daytime any more.

'Even I'd think twice about having babies these days,' I overheard Mum admit to Jessie recently. 'Imagine the climate in fifty years' time.'

I picture my aunt nodding: she's always had strong views on this subject.

'Another mouth to feed is not what this planet

needs,' she says, if anyone dares ask why she doesn't have children. 'Who'd want their kids inheriting a world that's getting hotter and hotter?'

It made me realise how fast everything is changing. Grown-ups like Mum can remember when the damage done by fossil fuels was only just becoming obvious. Even now, when we're living in forty degrees of heat, our air con and ice-cold fridges are only making the world hotter. And the saddest part of it is the poorest countries, with the smallest carbon footprints, are the ones suffering the most.

'D'you know America generates eighty times more carbon than Sierra Leone?' my aunt told me. It's a fact I've not forgotten.

Joel taps me on the arm. 'You still mad with Sasha?'

I blink. 'What?'

For the first time in ages it had honestly slipped my mind.

'You're going on holiday so cheer up, misery guts,' says Joel.

'D'you think something's wrong with Mum?' I reply, because that is what's bothering me.

'Dunno. It's probably the heat.'

I sigh. 'That's what Dad says.'

Realistically it could be any number of things: the

stress of the gardening business not making money, or being stuck inside all summer with us two. Sasha's cousin had cancer last year and lost all her hair, so I'm aware you don't have to be old to be seriously ill.

*

Outside Exeter station there's a bus idling and a few parked-up taxis, their windscreens glinting in the sun. The heat is so fierce I can smell the tarmac melting.

'Where *is* she?' Joel shields his eyes with his hand as he looks for Jessie.

'There!' I point. Our aunt is waiting in the only patch of shade. As she turns, sees us, her face piercings catch the light like stars.

'Welcome, travellers!' she cries, rushing over to throw her arms around us.

I've forgotten how much taller than Mum she is, and thinner. They barely look like sisters at all: our mum's short-haired and dark, Jessie's got copper-red hair down to her waist that she never brushes.

I hug her tightly. She smells like she always does, of patchouli and fusty clothes. I'm so glad to see her: everything feels better now, like a holiday *and* a birthday at the same time. When I pull away, I notice Joel turn his device off and tuck it in his back pocket. At last.

'Great to have you here, blessed niece, blessed nephew.' Jessie always calls us this.

Hugs done, I glance around for Jessie's car: there doesn't seem to be one.

'I sold it ages ago,' she explains. 'Got myself an electric bike. We'll have to catch the bus.'

Thankfully, the bus we need is one that's already here.

Once we're out of the city, the bus picks up speed. The trees are shimmering, drooping, and the fields, usually green and full of cows, are bare yellows and browns. A few miles into the ride Jessie's device goes off. It's the telltale ping-ping of the government alert, warning us the temperature has reached forty-two degrees.

'Again?' Joel groans.

'It's been like it every day this week,' Jessie confirms. 'And no end in sight, either.'

For once, I don't mind: at Jessie's there's nothing much else to do but paddle in the lake and sit in the shade. Just being here is already making me feel better. I'm glad we came.

*

The bus drops us at the top of a lane. From there we walk down a track that leads to Jessie's house. Thankfully there's some shade from the hedges, though the air is so hot it's hard to breathe. Even here, deep in the hills, the grass is almost white. It could be autumn already from the reds and golds of the trees. Happily everything else looks familiar: the little sky-blue box for post at the end of Jessie's drive, the wind chime in the tree, the boulder propping open the gate. I feel a rush of fondness for the place.

'Wait until you see what's happened to the lake,' Jessie says.

She calls the reservoir a lake – everyone does.

Truthwater Lake.

Shouldering our bags, we follow Jessie round to the front of the house. The garden is looking more overgrown than usual, the straggly plants and trees throwing more welcome shade across the path. Joel is just ahead of me, hurrying, because any moment now he'll get a glimpse of the lake through the apple trees, and Jessie's garden slopes right down to the water's edge. Already I can smell the muddy, silty murk of it that's so different from the sea back home. I walk faster, eager to get down there and wade in till the water covers my knees. It's going to feel wonderfully, refreshingly cold.

Joel stops so suddenly I walk into the back of him.
'Whoa!' he gasps. 'Where *is* the lake?'
I dodge round him to see it for myself.

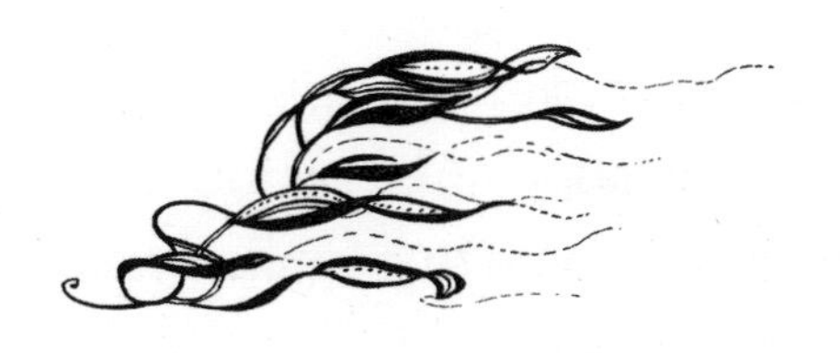

3.
SUMMER, 2032
POLLY

I must be looking in the wrong direction. The last time I was here the entire valley was underwater, yet most of what I'm seeing now is hard-baked mud, criss-crossed by old stone walls, all of it shimmering like a desert in the heat. It's only at the bottom of the valley, where the reservoir is deepest, that some water still remains. I'm stunned at what the heatwave has done.

'It looks so . . . *different*,' I manage to say.

The reservoir is supposed to reach from the concrete dam at one end of the valley to the sluice gates at the other. It's the sort of place people come to sail dinghies, to walk their dogs and eat picnics on the grass banks, or if it rains – *when* it rains – to buy cream teas and postcards in the shop at the dam end, near the car park. What's left of the reservoir is no bigger than two, maybe three swimming pools.

Jessie points to the stone walls. 'Strange, isn't it, to see the old village again?'

'There was a village here?' I've never heard this before.

'Syndercombe,' Jessie explains. 'Mentioned in the Domesday Book, apparently, but after the reservoir was built, they renamed the whole valley Truthwater.'

I wonder why.

'See my apple trees?' Jessie points behind us at her garden: this year there's not much fruit on the trees. 'They came from Syndercombe – a man took them from his own orchard and planted them up here. Couldn't bear to see them drown.'

'What happened to the people?' I ask, wiping sweat from my eyes.

'They had to move out and leave their homes behind.'

The stone walls, I see now, are in fact the outlines of houses. Those nearest to us are in a row as if they were once on the same street. In some of the walls you can still see spaces where ground-floor windows were. It's eerie. I wonder who lived here – real, actual people who went to school, grew vegetables in their gardens, had babies, pegged out washing to dry. It's a lost kingdom, a ghost village.

Jessie nods towards the bottom of the valley where water still lies.

'St Mary's, the old church, is under that lot,' she says.

Joel looks interested. 'Wow, must be deep there.'

'It is.' She smiles, wide-eyed, putting on her spooky-story voice. 'On a quiet winter's night you can still hear the bells ringing under the water.'

Joel grins. 'Awesome!'

'It isn't,' I blurt out. 'It's horrible.'

'It's only a story, angel,' Jessie says, gently.

Still, I feel quite choked up.

'Seeing the houses like this, it's really sad.'

'It's the past coming back to haunt us, that's what it feels like,' Jessie agrees, then glances at her old wristwatch and yelps. 'Ah, sweet heavens, my shift starts in half an hour. I'd better go.'

I must've looked momentarily lost because she tweaks my chin.

'Be happy, little one. You're on holiday. Now come inside and cool off.'

*

That night I can't sleep. Too much stuff is stomping around in my head. Mum's ill, Sasha and I aren't talking, and at the bottom of Jessie's garden is what remains of an old village. And it turns out the countryside *is* as hot as the city. Despite kicking off the sheet and flipping the pillow over so it's cool side up, I can't settle. By two o'clock I give up trying. Thinking it'll be cooler outside, I get out of bed, pull on shorts and T-shirt, grab a torch and go into the garden. There's a big dog fox under the apple trees, gulping down the scraps Jessie leaves out for them. The foxes are getting hungrier, she says, and tamer. Last week she caught one indoors sniffing about on her kitchen table.

Even outside, it's still way too hot. What I'd give to not feel sweaty and headachy. It's hard to remember ever being cold. I catch myself thinking about that night in the sea, the swimming part before everything went wrong. The water *did* feel amazing. I'd do anything to be that cool again, even – maybe – go swimming.

Don't, says the worry voice in my head. *You said you wouldn't, not after last time.*

But with no one here to talk me out of it, the idea takes hold. It's not just because I'm hot, or to prove something to my brother or to Sasha but because of what Jessie says is under the water. Perhaps it's possible to see the old church: I'd really like to have a look. My fear of deep water seems to have shifted into a strange, fizzing energy. The fox barely glances up as I tiptoe across the lawn.

At the water's edge, the lake looks oily black in the darkness. The air down here feels damp, almost cool. Above me the sky is aglitter with stars, and the half-moon, as yellow as a lemon slice, is bright enough to throw my shadow across the water. The excited fizzing is still there in the pit of my stomach. Yet for a moment, I dither, the old fear sneaking back. Should I really go in?

It's then the soft part of my foot catches something hard.

'Owww!' I wince, hopping on the spot.

I try to see what I've just stepped on. Despite the dark, I find it almost immediately and pick it up. It's long and narrow, the size of a large chocolate bar, but it weighs a lot more. I switch on the torch I brought with me.

What's in my hand appears to be a door handle. An old one. It's mud-encrusted, but the handle actually turns, making a gritty rasping sound. Perhaps it's from the old village, I think. And if it is, then whose front door did it open? Whose hand once gripped the handle? Who was the last person to ever close the door? My brain swoops and spins with possibilities.

I'm tempted to take the door handle to show Joel, but decide instead to bring him down here tomorrow, so he can see where I found it. As I go to lay it back on the ground, the handle catches in my belt hook. I can't untangle it, despite a few irritable moments trying. In the end I give up and tuck it in my pocket. I'll sort it later: right now, I'm here to swim.

Taking a big, bold breath, I walk into the water. It *is* cool, amazingly so, and it's this I try to concentrate on, not eels or sharks or piranhas. Though you hear stories all the time these days about wildlife getting confused by the weather and ending up in places they're not meant to be, like the foxes in Jessie's kitchen.

As the water reaches my waist, I'm almost used to how cool it feels. There's no pull against my legs, no warm or cold currents. The handle in my pocket isn't as heavy as I expected. I can do this, I tell myself. I just have to block out Joel's angry voice telling me I was drowning and Sasha saying I swam like a poodle. I say it over and over in my head: I can do this. Pushing off, I start to swim.

I head into the centre of the lake, where the church is supposed to be. The only noise is the soft swish-swish of my arms and legs moving through the water. To my surprise, swimming feels easier here than it does in the sea or at the pool. It gives me the confidence to keep going, and I do until a strange sensation takes hold. It's like I'm being pulled, very gently, downwards. I sense something underneath me. My foot brushes a hard surface.

I gulp, snatching my leg away, heart suddenly pounding. Something *is* down there. It's too dark to see what, but my imagination has more than enough ideas, all of them more terrifying than Jessie's church. My teeth are chattering. I knew it was stupid to come out here by myself.

I fumble for the torch around my neck: it's supposed to be waterproof, and thankfully, the light comes on, blindingly bright for a second. Then all I see is the lake gleaming back at me. Just below the surface, the water swirls like fog, greys and greens and a strange shade of almost-red, which is the colour of the soil in the local fields. It looks eerie and beautiful, like storm clouds.

Nothing's there, I tell myself, trying to calm down.

And it almost works. Just as I feel myself starting to relax my foot touches something again, something smooth and hard. I don't dare look: my dizzy brain isn't ready. I'm also becoming more aware of the door handle bumping against my hip.

Feeling along with my other foot, I then realise what this is, what I'm standing on. That ridge beneath my toes is the edge of a tile. Beyond it, more edges, more tiles. If I stretch my leg right down, I reach what feels like guttering. I am on a rooftop, of what I'm guessing must be the old church.

'Wow!' I gasp, though there's no one here to hear me. 'Oh wow!'

I can't wait to see Joel's face when I tell him. Or Sasha's.

Feeling braver, I point the torchlight into the water. It's so strange to be gazing down on a building like this when I should be looking up at it, my feet on dry land. It's as if I'm a bird or a fish or in another world entirely. In the beam of my torch, the roof is grey, covered in green algae, and beyond the roof, a door lintel, arched and important-looking with a row of apples carved into the wood.

Deeper still, I see the curve of a gravestone, then another topped with a stone urn. My guess was right: this *is* the church Jessie was talking about. The torch picks out huge gaps between the headstones: most of the graves are missing. What happened to the bodies in the coffins buried beneath, I wonder? Where do people go nowadays if they want to leave flowers on a loved one's grave? The sadness of it makes me shiver.

The water too has turned colder suddenly, and begins to swirl around me. It's time to go back. But as I try to swim to shore, the water tugs on my clothes so I can't move away. In my pocket, the door handle feels as if it's *turning*. Strangest of all is that I don't feel scared. I'm being pushed, pulled, guided somewhere, and wherever it is, I decide it's best to go with it. I let myself sink down. And down.

My chest tightens. I can't breathe. Panic comes over me, yet as quick as it comes, it's gone again. I seem to know exactly where I'm going now, and start to swim to the very bottom of the lake. The torch proves it's not so waterproof after all, and blinks and dies: I don't need it, anyway.

In the graveyard it's daylight bright, and though there's a blackbird singing, it doesn't feel weird at all. I'm aware of other noises too – a dog barking, sheep bleating, and a woman calling to me: 'Nellie? You realise what the time is, don't you?' and I know in my bones that my name isn't Polly any more, that I'm Nellie and I'm due to be somewhere, and I'll regret it for ever if I'm late.

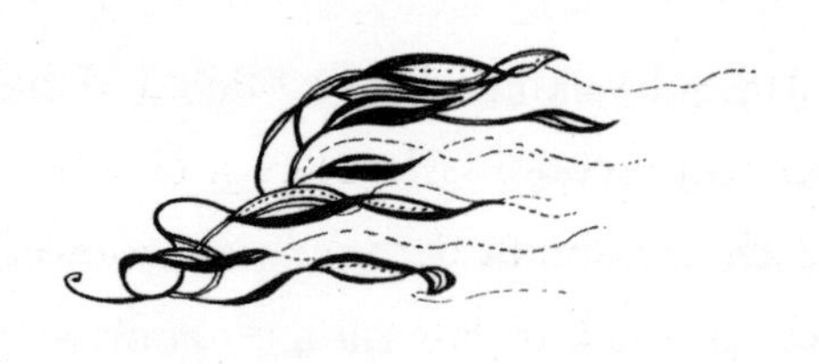

4.
WINTER, 1952
NELLIE

It was Saturday morning, and I'd woken early to the horrid feeling of damp bedsheets sticking to my skin. I wasn't ill, I didn't suppose, yet something had disturbed me. And so, by seven thirty, my pal Lena and I found ourselves wide awake, breakfasted and on our weekly trip to St Mary's churchyard. It was where my mam was buried, and having Lena with me made the visit that little bit more bearable.

'Imagine if Ma Blackwell was your mother, Nellie,' Lena said. 'You'd look like her. You'd have the hairy top lip and eyebrows that meet in the middle!'

I told her to stop it immediately, though in truth, it was our favourite game. We called it 'Mamas and Papas', and the rules were simple: you picked the most unlikely, unsuspecting grown-up and declared them the other person's parent. It never failed to make us snigger, especially in school assemblies or church services, when sniggering was most definitely not allowed.

Yet despite our daft game – or maybe because of it – Lena understood the importance of family. Though I wasn't the only sad person that week: King George had died a few days earlier, so the whole country was grieving.

Amongst the churchyard's clustered Celtic crosses and lopsided angels, Mam's headstone still looked painfully new, but it was a whole year ago now, and time had a sneaky habit of moving on. The first snowdrops were already in the hedgerows. A few early catkins, fat as caterpillars, promised spring was on its way.

That morning, though, it was still very much February. The frost lay hard on the ground, and we'd wrapped ourselves up in our thickest winter coats, woolly hats pulled low over our ears. Lena, who hated the cold, was stamping her feet against it.

'Flowers *again*!' I remarked, kneeling down to inspect the fresh bunch on Mam's grave.

Lena peered over my shoulder. 'Is there a card?'

There wasn't: there never was. But once a month, since Mam died, someone left yellow roses on her grave. It was always the same: six bright flowers wrapped in paper from the florist in town. I'd never discovered who they were from.

'It's a secret admirer,' reckoned Lena.

'Or my long-lost sister,' was my suggestion.

All we knew was that some nameless person placed the order each month, which the florist then brought to the churchyard. It was baffling. I was glad Mam had such cheering flowers, especially on dead-of-winter days like today, but I was itching to know who was sending them. Perhaps it was time for a new game called 'Who Sent the Flowers' instead.

Lena helped me to my feet.

'As I was saying, Nellie, you and Ma Blackwell—'

'Oh, must we?' I groaned, trying not to smile.

'But you'd look so similar, people would think you were sisters – no, wait, *twins*!'

A laugh exploded from my mouth just as Ma Blackwell herself came into the churchyard through the lychgate. She was still wearing her indoor pinny and had the flushed look of a person who'd run all the way here.

'Hope she didn't hear us,' I muttered guiltily.

Really I'd a lot to thank Ma Blackwell for. At first, when Mam passed away, I kept thinking it was all a big mistake. That someone so full of life could die of a simple tooth infection didn't make sense. Even on that last afternoon, when Mam told me: 'Don't ever be ordinary, Nell', I had supposed it was the fever talking and she'd be better in the morning.

Her dying made me an orphan. My father – I never knew him – had been killed in the war. Mam met him at the seaside when he was on shore leave. He'd proposed with a plastic ring from the amusement arcade, so the story went, promising they'd marry when he returned. She waved him off on the train, thinking him her fiancé, and never saw him again.

When Mam died I didn't know what was to become of me. I'd heard of orphans being sent off to school like a parcel on the understanding they'd never come home, not even in the holidays. Just as I was beginning to despair, Ma Blackwell offered me a bed at Combe Grange, where she lived with her husband, Mr Blackwell.

'But there's nothing wrong with my lungs,' I'd insisted.

I didn't mean to sound ungrateful, but Combe Grange's apple orchard was where people with tuberculosis were sent to recover. The half a dozen huts were painted cream and brown like smart garden sheds, each with a narrow bed and a wicker chair, so that the patients could sit out in the sweet country air. A pair of nurses from the new National Health Service would bicycle over every day to tend the sick, some of whom came from as far away as London.

Ma Blackwell's offer, though, was for a bed *inside* the house. She'd be feeding me too, and clothing me, which, with some things still on the ration, was very kind of her indeed. I just hoped she wouldn't be shocked by my appetite: for a small person I did eat rather a lot.

'Only pack one suitcase, please. I've not much extra room,' Ma Blackwell warned me.

That was the hardest part: sorting through a lifetime of things – clothes, books, favourite blankets, pictures, my first pair of shoes. Everything had a memory attached to it.

Yet I was thrilled to be sharing my room with another girl. Lena Gill was from London, sent here with tuberculosis in her left lung. She'd been living in a boarding house with her father, who was working all the hours on earth. The NHS sent her to the countryside for fresh air and rest, and she'd spent the last two months in the orchard in one of the huts. For the last stage of her recovery, she was being moved indoors.

In the short time it took us to bagsy beds and unpack our things, we were chatting like old pals. Lena wanted to know all about the famous swimmers whose pictures I'd stuck above my bed.

'She's my favourite,' I said, pointing to the newspaper cutting of a young woman in a swimming cap. Gertrude Ederle, an American, was the first woman to swim the English Channel in 1926.

Lena sighed dreamily. 'Must be cool to have a dream like that and make it happen.'

'*Totally* cool,' I agreed.

We were still talking at bedtime. It carried on like that every night, long after lights out. Sometimes I'd listen to Lena's breathing as she slept, terrified she might die too. Each morning we'd say our own little catchphrase.

'What's the story, morning glory?' This was Lena's line.

And mine: 'What's your tale, nightingale?'

Lena had come to England from India four years earlier with her father – she called him Baapu – when the government invited people from Commonwealth countries to help rebuild Britain after the war. She'd lived in the Punjab, in the countryside, so didn't much enjoy London.

'It's too stinky and noisy,' she said, wrinkling her nose.

Lena's dad was trying to set up his own clothes-making business. When he'd done so he'd send for Lena's mum – her mata – who was still in the Punjab.

'Life's quite dull, really,' Lena admitted. 'I go to

school, come home, cook dhal. Poor Baapu's so tired he barely speaks.'

'Must be lonely,' I said, though the dhal, when she explained it, sounded delicious.

'Baapu's doing his best for us. But I'm a Punjabi, not a Londoner. I miss my mata, you know?'

I did know. I felt it every day, that emptiness when the most important person in your life wasn't there. Really, we were lucky to have Ma Blackwell, who, though not especially motherly, cared for us in her own way.

Like now, in the churchyard, when I'd clearly forgotten something important.

'Nellie, you do realise what the time is, don't you?' Ma Blackwell gasped, holding her side as if she had a stitch. 'And where you're meant to be?'

The truth was, I didn't.

The church clock showed it was five past eight. I'd fed the chickens, and Perry and Sage – Mr Blackwell's pair of beautiful working Clydesdales – made my bed, and laid out my costume and towel for later, because Saturday afternoons were swimming lesson time at Minehead lido: the highlight of my week. I couldn't think what we'd forgotten.

'Oh!' Lena said, suddenly. 'Sorry, it went straight out of my head.'

Hardly able to speak for grinning, she explained that a swimming coach – 'A famous one, Nellie, a celebrity!' – was coming to the lido to scout for 'exceptional' talent. Captain Farley had rounded up his best students for the special session that was happening today at nine thirty.

'How do you know?' I cried. 'Who told you?'

'Captain Farley in the post office yesterday, when I was cashing my postal order.'

Every week Lena's dad sent what money he could spare for her keep.

'*Yesterday?*' That was almost a full day ago. It amazed me how Lena could forget something *this* important.

'Captain Farley said to tell you,' Lena went on. 'He's coming to pick you up in his car. He's taking you himself!'

'*Me?*' I was thrilled, until it dawned on me that I'd be going alone. 'Aren't you coming too?'

Lena shook her head. 'Oh, I might sit this one out. My chest's a bit tight today.'

Really, Lena only came to the Saturday club because I'd gushed about it, and Ma Blackwell agreed a spot of exercise might build her strength after being ill. She wasn't a serious swimmer like me. It was my dream to be a professional one day. I was trying hard *not* to be ordinary and hoped my mam would be proud.

Mam had known the captain, working twice a week for him as a sort of housekeeper at Hadfield Hall, where he lived. I'd tag along sometimes, and while she did her chores I'd sit on the back step making daisy chains for the captain's spaniels. Very occasionally I'd be allowed inside for tea on the understanding that I'd be quiet and not eat too much cake.

Yet the idea of going in the captain's car, of driving the sixteen long miles to Minehead trying to think of what to say, terrified me.

'You'd better come with me, Lena!' I pleaded.

Lena laughed. 'Don't be a daftie, Nell!'

'I mean it.'

Ma Blackwell, who'd once tried to make me swallow cod liver oil and knew better than to battle my stubborn streak head-on, made a suggestion.

'That car of the captain's—' she said.

'A Hillman Minx, newish but nothing fancy,' Lena confirmed. Coming from the city, she knew far more about cars than I did.

'Is it big enough to take the both of you?' Ma Blackwell replied. 'Because if you ask nicely the captain might take Lena along for the ride.'

Captain Farley, who ran his swimming classes with army-level discipline, believed children should know their place, which, in his eyes, was somewhere beneath horses and spaniels in life's pecking order. If he'd chosen me – only me – to go to the session, then it wasn't up for discussion. Yet that didn't put me off.

Back at home I grabbed my swimming things, and Lena, who wore her hair in a single braid long enough to sit on, said she'd plait my hair specially for the occasion. By the time the captain's car pulled up, I had hair as neat as a horse's tail, and was waiting on the front step with Lena.

'What's all this?' Captain Farley looked puzzled as he got out of the car. 'It's *Nellie* I've come for.'

'Please, sir, Lena's my lucky mascot,' I said.

'I am,' Lena agreed. 'She won't swim without me.'

Which was a bit of an exaggeration, but after glancing at his watch, the captain miraculously relented. 'Very well. Get in. No time for dawdling.'

We clambered into the back seat as giddy as a pair of foals. Driving out of the village in a car was a thrill all of its own, especially when we saw Janet and Ruthie Steggs from our school class coming out of the post office, and the surprise on their faces as we went past, waving.

Feeling braver with Lena next to me, I asked the captain about the mysterious celebrity coach.

'Are they really famous, sir?' I asked.

'Indeed. And coming all the way from America to see us.'

I wriggled with excitement. Lena had forgotten to mention *this* detail, which was by far the juiciest part of it all, because my all-time swimming hero came from America.

'It's not . . .' I gulped. '. . . Gertrude Ederle, the Channel swimmer, is it?'

The captain gave a rare chuckle. 'Not a bad guess, but no, it's not Miss Ederle.'

'Oh. Who is he, then?'

'*She*, Nellie,' the captain corrected me. 'Mrs Lamb is a she, and a champion in open-water swimming. She's made a name for herself – and a considerable fortune – these past few years, all simply from being a swimmer.'

'My!' Though I'd not heard of her, she did sound impressive. 'Will she be training us?'

Secretly, I hoped she would. It wasn't that the captain was a bad coach, but he had a loud parade-ground voice, and when he lost his temper – which was often – his face went alarmingly red.

'She'll be making a selection for a very special project. She's looking for stamina, the ability to endure distance and cold,' the captain replied. 'And those are your particular strengths, Nellie.'

I nodded. I'd regularly swim long, gruelling distances at the lido – often for hours at a time – and was getting quite a taste for it.

'Though I should warn you,' the captain added. 'Mrs Lamb will be selecting only one person. You might be *my* top swimmer, but you'll still have to battle it out.'

I'd already guessed who I'd be up against from our club: Maudie Jennings, Timmy Valentine, Jim Sutton, Bob Blake. I'd have my work cut out. So would Mrs Lamb: there wasn't much to choose between us, in terms of our swimming ability.

Still, Lena and I shared a big old grin. The others hadn't been given a ride in Captain Farley's car or been called his top swimmer, which surely meant I was in with a fighting chance.

5.
WINTER, 1952
NELLIE

Saturday mornings at the lido were always busy. The pool was on Minehead seafront and boasted a thirty-three-foot-high diving tower and crystal-clear water pumped in from the beach just across the road: I never knew how they did it, when the sea itself was the colour of strong tea. But it was a superb pool for swimming, and regularly hosted national championships and galas, some of which I'd already taken part in.

We arrived to a crowd of pushchairs, prams, crying babies and little kids in woolly mittens clutching their parents' hands, and had to join a long queue to go in. The promise of open-air swimming in unheated water – in February – obviously hadn't put people off. By now I was a flutter of nerves. Once through the turnstile, it was some relief to see Timmy Valentine, Bob Blake and Jim Sutton, waiting with their kitbags.

'You got the nod too, eh?' Bob greeted us with a pally wink.

'And a lift in the gaffer's car, by the look of it,' muttered Jim, who was fiercely competitive.

Captain Farley quickly ushered the boys off to get ready. In our changing room, we found Maudie Jennings, the only other girl member of our club, and who acted like a big sister to us younger ones. She was wearing her competition costume today – navy with white piping around the edges.

'Morning, kittens,' she said, which was what she always called us. 'Any sign of the lady herself out there?'

'Mrs Lamb? Not yet,' I replied.

I got changed quickly. I'd feel less nervous once I was in the water – I always did – but I still wasn't sure what Mrs Lamb was choosing one of us *to do*. Was it for a competition? The county team?

'D'you know what Mrs Lamb's special project is?' I asked Maudie.

'Must be something amazing,' Lena added. 'Everyone's acting like she's a queen.'

Maudie stared at us, agog. 'You don't *know*?'

We shook our heads.

'She . . .' Maudie took a dramatic breath, '. . . swam the English Channel in world-record time in 1928. She's won big sponsorship deals, been on magazine covers, travelled the wor—'

'She swam the English Channel?' I interrupted, because this was the part that interested me. I was annoyed at myself for not knowing her name.

'Yes, kitten, keep up,' Maudie chattered on. 'Her sponsors are on the lookout for a kid swimmer to take up the challenge. They want someone to do it this summer. The captain asked her along to see if any of us lot might be good enough.'

'Wow!' Lena exclaimed.

I was in a daze.

Captain Farley called swimming the English Channel a 'swimmer's Everest'. Only the very best attempted it. One day, I wanted to try – that had long been my dream – but as a grown-up, in my twenties, like Gertrude Ederle. I'd never considered that a *kid* could swim the Channel. Just the thought made my heart flip. Here was a chance to do something completely and utterly *not* ordinary. I could almost hear Mam saying those words.

'I hope Mrs Lamb picks me,' I said, straight out.

Maudie's swimming hat made a snapping sound as she tucked in the last lock of hair.

'Then you'll have to beat me and Jim, won't you?' she answered.

She didn't call me kitten again.

*

Mrs Lamb was waiting for us at the poolside. Despite the din of the other Saturday swimmers, her voice carried, as shrill as a whistle: it was this I noticed first, then her shoes. She was dressed exactly like I'd imagine a wealthy person would dress – immaculate hair, pearls and the most ludicrously sky-high heels.

'Ah, the girls.' Mrs Lamb greeted Maudie and me, glancing at Lena. 'You're not swimming?'

'Me? Not likely!' Lena backed away, reappearing moments later in the spectators' gallery. Amongst the fathers reading their Saturday papers, she took a seat and gave me an encouraging wave. That settled me, as did the familiar pool smell, the sparkle of the water, seeing our boys in their one-pieces, hands tucked in armpits, serious and ready.

Really, I told myself, it was much like a normal Saturday session. The only difference was Mrs Lamb being in charge, and Captain Farley in the background, silent, his eyes fixed on our special visitor. There was no introduction from Mrs Lamb herself, no friendly hullos.

'The first point I'm going to make will surprise you—' She stopped as a boy emerged from the changing rooms and joined our group. 'Oh, we've one more swimmer?'

An outbreak of nudging followed: none of us knew who the new addition was.

'Simmer down!' the captain barked. 'This is our new club member, who I *wasn't* expecting to join us today.'

He gave the boy a frosty glare.

'I'm terribly sorry, Mr Farley,' the boy answered, not exactly at ease himself. 'But my father said—'

'It's *Captain* Farley, young man,' Captain Farley interrupted irritably. 'And you're taking up Mrs Lamb's valuable time.'

Once Mrs Lamb began talking again, we were quickly transfixed. She told us Channel swimming was set to become the newest, biggest craze: in America, where she lived, every swimmer wanted to try the English Channel. It was up there with the Catalina Channel, off the Californian coast, as one of the world's toughest swims.

'Though the English Channel *is* colder,' she pointed out.

As well as the swim itself, which no child had yet managed, she talked about the fame a successful attempt would bring. And dollars. A major chewing gum manufacturer was offering sponsorship worth thousands for the lucky child. This was an opportunity that would change a person's life.

'My chosen swimmer will have stamina and . . .' She paused dramatically. 'That all-important star quality.'

There was also the issue of timing. Though it was more common to swim the Channel in late summer when the sea was at its warmest, she and the sponsor were hoping for a date in June.

'The sooner we do our swim, the better. We don't want anyone else stealing our thunder, do we?' she said with steely determination.

I had to admit, I was in awe. By the time she'd finished talking, I'd forgotten the new boy entirely until she ordered us into the water, in pairs. Looking around for Maudie, my usual partner, I saw she'd gone with Jim. The new boy and I were the only two left.

'Looks like you're lumped with me,' the boy said. 'Awfully sorry.'

'You *are* a decent swimmer, aren't you?' I asked, because I didn't want him holding me back.

He shrugged. 'I suppose I'm all right.'

He looked harmless enough – about my age, thickset, with freckly shoulders and curly brown hair. But my heart was sinking. Only one swimmer would be chosen. It was bound to be Maudie or Jim. They both already looked super confident as they strolled down to the deep end.

'I'm Nathaniel Clatworthy, by the way,' the boy said as we climbed into the pool.

As names went, it felt a beat too long and a tad too grown-up.

'Crikey, don't you have a nickname?'

'Umm . . . Natty? No . . . actually, Nate.' It was obvious he'd made it up on the spot. 'And you are?'

I spat into my goggles before putting them on.

'Nellie Foster,' I said.

*

'Nate', it turned out, was a great name to scream at the top of your lungs. Over the next hour, I'd plenty of opportunity, as Mrs Lamb made us swim laps of the pool in a relay race that pitted us against the two other pairs.

'Left, Nate!'

'Keep going, Nate! He's right on your tail!'

And failing all else, '*Nnnnnnnaaaatttttteeeee!*'

To my surprise, Nate could indeed swim. His style was unfussy, at times a bit clumsy, but it worked. He wasn't as fast as Maudie on his leg of the relay, yet he caught up easily when she tired.

The next race was backstroke, my favourite. I loved how the water surged against my skull, my shoulders twisting, the flipper-kick of my feet. I was paired against Bob and won easily. From the spectators' gallery, Lena cheered louder than anyone.

'You're a champ in the making, you are!' Bob said as we caught our breath at the pool's edge.

It was sporting of him to say so, but it was becoming obvious who'd caught Mrs Lamb's attention. It wasn't that Nate was the quickest or had the best technique. Yet when he moved through the water there was a real power to him that was like watching Mr Blackwell's Clydesdales at work. I didn't think I swam like that: Jim and Maudie didn't, either. If star quality was what Mrs Lamb wanted, then Nate was the one who had it: none of us could take our eyes off him.

At the session's end we were sent to get changed, before returning to the poolside to hear Mrs Lamb's verdict. A little hopeful part of me knew I'd swum well. Lena, giving me an enthusiastic thumbs up, seemed to think so. Captain Farley too gave me a brief nod of approval.

Still, as Mrs Lamb began addressing us, my heart raced. Silently I begged her to pick me, for her to say my name out loud: I wanted it for me and for Mam, so fiercely it almost scared me.

But it wasn't to be.

'The swimmer with the most potential, in my view,' she announced, 'is Nathaniel Clatworthy.'

Immediately, Jim burst into tears. I choked mine down, as best I could, but I'd never felt so disappointed about anything in my life.

*

On the way back in the car, Captain Farley offered us each a mint humbug. I didn't want mine and gave it to Lena.

'Damn that Clatworthy boy for taking your place, Nellie!' the captain fumed.

'Who is he, anyway?' Lena wanted to know, a humbug in each cheek.

The captain took so long to answer I thought he hadn't heard the question. Then, in a strange, tight voice, he said: 'You'll find out soon enough.'

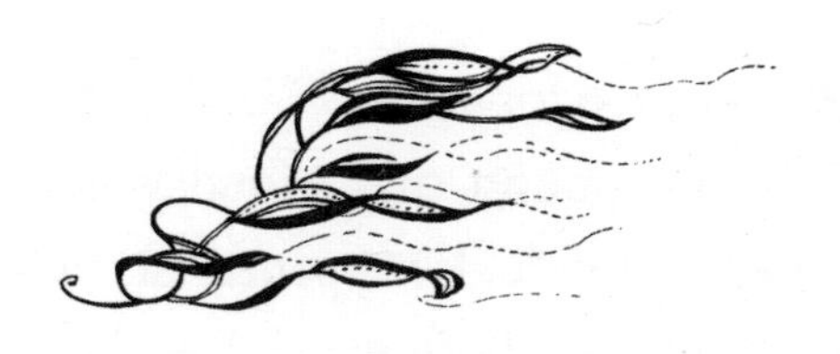

6.
Early Spring, 1952
Nellie

At first the disappointment was hard to shake off. I wasn't the only one suffering, either: on Monday morning on our way to class we passed Maudie waiting for her bus to the big school in town.

'Who *is* that new boy?' she demanded, still fuming. ''Cause he don't sound local to me.'

'I dunno,' I admitted.

Neither Lena nor I knew anything about Nate Clatworthy, though I'd a dreadful feeling he might turn up in our class today, like a grim repeat of Saturday at the pool. All morning, I kept an anxious eye on the door. Our teacher, Miss Setherton, noticed I wasn't paying attention, and made me stand up at the front to write spellings on the blackboard, which didn't go well. But by lunchtime, there was still no Nate Clatworthy.

'He's too good for us,' was Lena's view.

In the playground that Monday most of the talk was about what had happened at swimming club. Tim and Bob were both very relieved to not be picked by Mrs Lamb.

'Twenty-odd miles of freezing sea? The lido's cold enough!' Bob said with a shudder.

'Yeah, but when you reached the other side, you'd be the first kid our age to do it,' I countered. 'And that would be the absolute business.'

'I wouldn't mind the money,' admitted Tom. 'Though they'd have to pay me millions.'

Personally, I'd have done it for the glory.

*

Now satisfied Nate wasn't coming to our school, I spent the next few days in class deep in daydreams. I'd imagine Mrs Lamb calling my name instead of Nate's. Or I'd wonder if he was swimming every day, and if so, how far? Was he eating special food, learning special techniques? How did it feel to be picked for such an incredible challenge? Had he been to France before?

Even Miss Setherton rapping on my desk with her ruler didn't snap me out of it for long.

I simply could not stop thinking about the swim. I envied Nate Clatworthy so much it hurt. The more time passed, the more I wanted to be the first child to swim the Channel. I even began thinking up ludicrous schemes to oust him from Mrs Lamb's favour.

'Maybe he's a spy,' I suggested to Lena. 'Or a criminal. We should follow him and see what he's up to.'

'Or put chillies in his swimming costume' was her idea. She grew pots of red and green ones in our kitchen window. Her mum had sent the seeds from India. Chilli scrambled eggs was one of our favourite breakfasts.

I couldn't help but laugh. 'You can't do that!'

'Why not?' she said, all innocent. 'He's bad news, he is.'

The daft game of Mamas and Papas forgotten, we now made it our mission to find out all we could about Nate Clatworthy. We started by asking Mrs Lee at the post office because she knew everything. She told us he didn't go to school but had a tutor at home.

'That's super posh,' I remarked.

So was the house where the Clatworthys lived: a handsome Victorian villa in the next valley where the stables had been turned into a row of garages.

'Bet his dad's got a fancy car,' sighed Lena.

'Some people get all the luck, don't they?' I said, thoroughly fed up. 'I know it's not about the money, but he doesn't even need it.'

'I definitely like him even less now,' Lena agreed.

*

On Wednesday, on the way home from school, Lena tapped her knuckles on my forehead.

'Ouch!' I cried. 'What was that for?' Though, to be fair, I had been thinking about Channel swimming again.

'You haven't been listening to a word I've said, have you?'

'Have.'

'What've I just said about the meeting today?' she asked, testing me. 'The one the whole village is going to, in the village hall?'

'What meeting?'

Lena gave me a very long look. 'Bet you didn't hear Mr Blackwell at breakfast asking us to do Perry and Sage so he can go, did you?'

'Yes, I did.' Though I'd clean forgotten it until now.

'Thought you'd at least remember who's called the meeting,' Lena said. 'A Mr *Clatworthy*?'

'Oooooh!' I stopped walking. 'Nate's dad?'

She nodded.

'What's the meeting about?'

Lena grinned. 'You know, I've an idea Mr Clatworthy's a famous film director and he's looking for somewhere to set his next film.'

'Yeah!' I gasped, thrilled we might be on to something. 'That's why Mrs Lamb chose Nate, because of his dad's connections! She wanted someone with star quality who could be really famous!'

'And having a dad who worked in the movies would be a big help.'

'What time's the meeting?'

'Ah.' Lena's face fell. 'It's adults only, so they'll never let us in. Anyway, we've got the horses to do.'

'I know that, you great chump,' I said, linking her arm with mine and walking on.

'So why're you looking at me like that?'

'You'll see.'

*

Swapping our school shoes for boots, we went to the top field to meet Mr Blackwell, where he was working the horses. He was clearing a hedge, the trailer stacked with dead wood and brambles. Perry saw us coming and gave a throaty neigh. He was my favourite of the two horses; it amazed me how a creature so big could take carrot bits from your hand so daintily. And if you had no treats on offer straight away, like today, he'd check your pockets with his top lip.

'That time already, is it?' Mr Blackwell asked, stepping back from the hedge. He didn't wear a watch, claiming proper country folks told the time by the angle of the sun. Though today it was grey and cold with no sun to speak of.

'Better hurry or you'll not get a seat,' Lena told him. 'I've heard it's going to be packed out.'

She'd heard nothing of the sort, but Mr Blackwell, who loved an occasion, was at the horses' heads in a flash and leading them back down the hill.

In the yard, Ma Blackwell was waiting for her husband. She had her coat on already, her best hat pinned in place.

'There you are,' she tutted.

'Here I am, Missus,' he replied, throwing the reins to me.

They went off to the village hall as eager as two people going to a tea dance. It was all rather intriguing, and made me more determined to find out what Mr Clatworthy was up to.

'It might not be a film, but he's here for some reason,' agreed Lena.

Once we'd untacked the horses down to their bridles, we rode them bareback to the ford. It was the horses' usual routine. Mr Blackwell swore the ice-cold water was good for cooling their legs after a hard day, and the horses knew it meant their work was over. They could be skittish and silly, and start pawing at the water: you had to watch it then, because if they rolled you'd get thrown off or flattened underneath.

Today, they were calm, but even when they weren't I still loved doing the horses. It was their sweet smell, their solid, armchair bulk, and the way they looked at you with such honest faces. At first, Lena had been terrified of Perry and Sage. But last summer, bit by bit, I'd taught her to ride – or at least to stay on top long enough to get to the ford and back.

Now, the horses drank deeply, then stood, heavy headed, water dripping from their horsey beards. In the hedge behind us a thrush was singing into the dusk. Somewhere in the distance, I could hear the rumble of a car's engine. Sage heard it too, her head swinging up, ears pricked.

The car came into view on the road above the village. It was travelling at considerable speed, its headlights zigzagging down the hillside, picking out gorse bushes, grazing sheep, the reddish-brown soil of the valley.

'That's not Captain Farley, is it?' I said.

'Nope. Wrong type of car.'

Even from this distance I understood what Lena meant: the car's engine sounded deeper; its shape was long and low to the ground. Not many people round here had a car, never mind a fancy one. The road down to the village was little more than a stony track. The grocery van might risk it if the weather was dry, but everyone else came and went on foot, bicycle, horseback or cart.

According to Lena, in the future everyone would own a car, and tracks like ours would be smoothed over with tarmac, the trees and hedgerows cut down to make a wider, straighter road. It would make our little village look like a town, and I couldn't imagine that at all. Yet this particular driver seemed to think he *was* in a town, and driving way too fast. At the final bend, when it was already too late, the car tried to slow.

Lena groaned. 'He's not going to stop, is he?'

I felt a flash of fear.

'Go! Go! Go!' I cried, urging Perry further downstream.

Lena drummed her heels against Sage's sides.

We only just got the horses away from the ford in time. As the car hit the water, spray went everywhere. There was a crunching sound like metal scraping rock, and the grinding of brakes. The horses snorted, side-stepping into each other. I grabbed handfuls of Perry's mane and held on tight, as the car roared past only a few feet from us.

'Slow down, you idiot!' Lena yelled at the driver.

In the blur of water and horse and car, I glimpsed the driver's face. In the passenger seat beside him was a boy I recognised. The car was through the ford and gone before I could react.

'That was flipping close!' Lena slumped forward, hugging Sage's neck. 'What sort of person drives like *that*?'

'Nate Clatworthy.' I said his name with a new level of disdain. 'Not driving, obviously, but he was in the car.'

'That must've been Mr Clatworthy, then.' Lena whistled. 'You know what type of car that was, don't you?'

I didn't. But Lena was clearly going to tell me.

'A Jaguar SS. Seriously expensive,' she said, eyes wide. 'Maybe he *is* a film director.'

The encounter had left both horses soaked through and jumpy. They were also well aware of what normally followed a trip to the ford – a trough of bran and oats and a rub-down in a nice warm stable. They were glad to be heading home. The problem was we weren't, not yet. My bright idea was to ride up to the village hall, where, from the back of a giant of a horse, we'd be able to see in through the windows. The trouble was our route to the hall took us straight past the gate into our yard.

I'd all good intentions, driving Perry on with my heels and seat. And he was responding, head up, stride brisk, listening to my commands. Yet at the last minute, he veered left towards Combe Grange, almost sending me over his shoulder. There, he stopped dead, and refused to go any further. I tried everything – heels, threats, promises of carrots – but he'd had enough. And if he'd had enough, so too had Sage. There was no arguing with eighteen hands of horse.

By the time we'd fed Perry and Sage and reached the hall, it was dark and the meeting was well under way.

'Bet Nate's been allowed in,' I said, crossly.

Paraffin lamps burned brightly at the windows, and though the door was closed, the walls were thin, corrugated tin, making it possible to catch snatches of what the now infamous Mr Clatworthy was saying, though it didn't sound very interesting. He was talking about water pipes.

I pulled a face at Lena. 'Is that what he's here for? *Pipes?*'

'Guess we can forget about the film director idea,' she replied, disappointed.

We couldn't hear much after that: it had started to rain, and the rattle of it on the tin roof drowned Mr Clatworthy's voice. Lena suggested going home. As we went back down the lane, discussing another of our favourite topics – what was for tea – I almost walked straight past Nate. He was on his knees, being sick in the hedge.

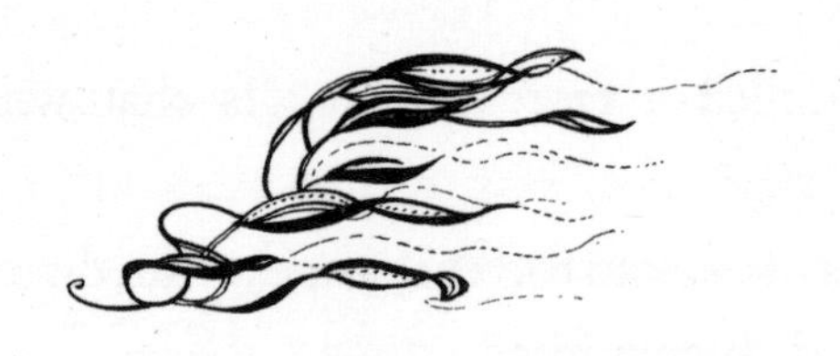

7.
EARLY SPRING, 1952
NELLIE

I should've asked Nate if he was all right. But I wasn't feeling especially friendly. Nor was Lena, who, after her own long illness, didn't have much patience with sick people.

'You again,' I said, keeping my distance from the figure crouched by the roadside.

Unsteadily, Nate got to his feet. In the village hall light he looked ghastly: there was sick all down the front of his coat, and not a drop of the star quality Mrs Lamb prized so highly. It was, I had to admit, rather satisfying.

'Ugh!' Lena pinched her nose. 'You smell revolting!'

'Well, *you* smell like a stable yard!' Nate shot back. His face crumpled, and he turned away as if he was trying not to cry.

I didn't know what to do. It was raining hard, and I wanted to get home – and Lena was right: he *did* smell awful. Yet though Nate Clatworthy was my least favourite person, he was quite poorly.

'Should we fetch someone?' I asked.

'No, don't do that,' he answered, whip quick. 'I'll be tip-top in a sec. It's being in Dad's car – I get sick every time.'

'Not surprised,' Lena remarked. 'He's one heck of a dangerous driver.'

'He is,' I agreed, still cross about it. 'You know he nearly killed us – and the horses – at the ford?'

Nate's chin wobbled, tears still threatening. 'I was about to throw up, that's why he was going so fast. He'd murder me if I did it in his car.'

'Well, it *is* a very decent car.' Lena narrowed her eyes at him. 'So if your dad's not a film director, why's he here?'

'He's obviously not,' I added, quickly. 'Not if he's talking about water pipes.'

'A film director?' Nate looked confused. 'No, he's from the South West Water Board.'

'Oh. Is that *all*?'

It was, all told, disappointingly dull, though I supposed it explained the pipes.

Lena yawned into her hand.

'Well, Nate, we won't keep you,' she said, and pulled at my arm. It was our turn to make tea tonight and we'd not settled on cheese on toast or oxtail soup.

But Nate kept talking, fast and nervous.

'You won't know this yet but the water board has bought this whole valley. That's why Father's here tonight, to break the news to the village. I only came along because Eddie – he's my little brother – wouldn't stop crying at home and it—'

'Hang on!' I stopped him, thinking I'd misheard. 'Someone's bought our valley?'

'That's the long and short of it, yes,' Nate replied.

'Yeah, right! Bet they've bought the village too, and the school and the church and all the houses,' Lena finished with a snort. 'Pull the other one, Clatworthy!'

'No one would sell, even if it was true,' I said confidently, thinking of the Blackwells, whose house and land had been in their family for generations. It was a ridiculous idea.

'It *is* the truth,' Nate insisted. 'It's called a compulsory purchase order. The people who live here don't have a choice. Damn shame, I know.'

I didn't know what a compulsory wotsit was: nor, from the look on her face, did Lena. But something told me Nate wasn't lying. I felt prickly and hot, suddenly.

'Go on, then!' I cried. 'Amaze us! What's your water board going to do with our valley? Turn it into a holiday camp?'

Lena laughed.

Nate glanced at us both. He'd gone pale again.

'They're building a reservoir. The towns around here need more fresh water, and your valley is the best place for it because . . . well . . .'

He stopped as the village hall's door swung open. The meeting was over. Lantern light and what appeared to be the entire adult population of Syndercombe spilled down the steps: Mrs Lee, who ran the post office, Reverend Matthews, Miss Setherton, Mr Smythe the master of the local hunt, Captain Farley, the Blackwells. Everyone was talking over each other, finishing each other's sentences, arguing, considering.

'—can't believe they can do that, sell our homes from under us.'

'He's offering decent compensation—'

'—chance of a fresh start after the war—'

'One of them new houses in town would suit us, eh, Derek?'

'All that water, though, and Syndercombe underneath. I can't picture it.'

'Best not to then, Marge. Think of it coming out of a tap, and straight into your kettle.'

Everyone was stirred up, and no wonder if what Nate had just told us was true. Just for a second, the swimmer in me marvelled at having a freshwater lake on our doorstep: I could go open-water swimming every day!

Then I heard the word 'flood'.

And Ma Blackwell did something I'd never seen before: she burst into tears. A few people, made awkward by it, turned away. Mr Blackwell put an arm around her shoulders. Mrs Lee passed her a hanky. Since we were meant to be at home getting the tea, Lena and I shrank back into the shadows.

'How can they flood us out of our homes? *How?*' Ma Blackwell sobbed.

It wasn't the sort of question that needed an answer, though Captain Farley tried.

'From what the water board chap said, they'll build a dam down by Crowsfoot Farm, then reroute the river up at Marley's Head. The school will clear out first, then the churchyard, then us . . .' He trailed off, smoothing his moustache wistfully like he did when people mentioned the Great War.

'Blimey, how do you clear a churchyard?' Lena whispered.

I didn't know. But if it meant I couldn't visit Mam and her mystery yellow roses any more, then I didn't like the sound of it.

*

At supper, no one had much of an appetite. Ma Blackwell, who was strict about food waste, scraped our half-full plates into the pig-swill bucket without a word. Normally, after clearing up, we'd listen to the wireless by the fire, or play rummy for the tops off the lemonade bottles, which we'd then trade for sweets at the post office. But tonight Mr Blackwell put on his best corduroy jacket and said he was off to the White Lion.

'On a Wednesday, John?' Ma Blackwell's knitting needles went silent. 'That in't usual.'

'These in't usual times, my love,' he replied.

When he'd gone, Ma Blackwell went to the kitchen. From behind the jars of pickled walnuts, cucumbers, red cabbage and shallots, she produced a brand-new bar of Bournville chocolate. Lena winked at me: we knew all too well where she kept her secret chocolate stash, and would often take it in turns to sniff the bar through its paper.

'Chocolate's very good for shock,' Ma Blackwell told us with authority, and proceeded to snap the bar into three.

We ate our chocolate slowly, quietly, savouring its sweetness.

'Will they really flood the village?' Lena wondered.

'That's the plan,' answered Ma Blackwell. 'Though it won't be happening till June at the earliest.'

'How will they do it?' I dared to ask.

'The whole village is to empty by the sixteenth of June: the deadline's two in the morning.' Ma Blackwell tutted. 'Though I ask you, who's going to be moving house in the middle of the night?'

'What about the flooding?' Because in my head I pictured a giant tidal wave surging down the valley.

'They do it slowly, so the man said. It takes months, which I s'pose gives us time to get used to it.'

'I won't ever get used to it,' I declared.

'It is mind-boggling, you're right,' Ma Blackwell agreed. 'Twenty billion gallons of water, Mr Clatworthy said. Tis going to be a big old reservoir. And deep too. Has to be, to cover St Mary's spire and the chimneys at Hadfield Hall.'

I couldn't imagine it. Even to me, so happy in deep water, the idea of everything being flooded was beyond strange. Some things were meant to be underwater – fish, shipwrecks, swimming-pool tiles – but not a whole village and all its buildings. Not my mam lying in her grave.

'You can't just pick up a village and put it somewhere else,' I insisted.

'Seems you can, pet,' Ma Blackwell replied sadly. 'If you've enough money and enough power, and enough people in the towns needing fresh water, then that's the priority, not our village.'

But if our homes were being flooded for the reservoir, where would we go? What would happen to me – and to Lena? My whole world felt suddenly very shaky indeed.

'Will I be coming with you when you leave, Ma Blackwell?' I asked, wanting reassurance.

She started knitting again, needles clacking at speed. 'If it can be afforded, dear.'

I'd hoped for a straightforward *yes*, and was taken aback.

'*Afforded?* You mean I'm too expensive?'

Ma Blackwell gave me one of her killer frowns. 'Now then, it all costs money, Nellie – food, clothes, all this to-ing and fro-ing to the swimming pool each week.'

My heart froze. 'You're sending me to the orphanage, aren't you?'

'I never said that, no!' she cried.

'What about Lena?' I was starting to really worry now.

Ma Blackwell looked from me to Lena. '*You'll* be going back to London, missy, to your father.'

Lena yelped. 'But—'

'No buts about it. Your chest cleared up months ago. I should've insisted on it then.'

'I want to be with Nellie,' Lena begged. 'I'm no trouble, am I?'

Ma Blackwell gave her an arch look but seemed to soften. 'Maybe you could stay on till the June deadline – *if*, and only if, your father agrees to it.'

She meant if he kept paying. It was only a small amount, but at least he was sending something towards her keep.

'Oh, he will!' Lena replied earnestly. I hoped she was right: his most recent payment had been less than usual, and she hadn't known why.

'But I warn you, girls,' Ma Blackwell reminded us. 'When we move, it'll be a fresh start for everyone.'

*

I was out of sorts for the rest of the evening. All year I'd lived with the Blackwells and Lena: a whole year of being part of a warm, busy, bustling family. I couldn't bear the thought of losing that – or Lena. That night as we brushed our teeth, side by side at the kitchen sink, Lena and I were both fighting back the tears.

'I don't want you to go,' I wailed.

'Nor do I.' Lena spat into the sink with force. 'I want to be here with you, Nell. I hate it in the city. Anyway, Ma Blackwell can't *make* me go back.'

'Can't she?' I wasn't so sure. Ma Blackwell was as strong as Perry and Sage, and twice as formidable. And right now, it felt as if she held both our fates in the balance.

We went up to bed in silence, quickly changing into our nightgowns and diving in under the bedclothes because our room was always freezing cold. As I lay in bed, the sheets slowly warming, I thought more about what Ma Blackwell had said – or not said.

The truth was, raising a child cost money. The Blackwells had been very kind to take me in when Mam died, when clearly I was an expense they could barely afford. They were responsible for me – for Lena too while she was under their roof. Had we been their daughters or nieces it would've been different. But we weren't the Blackwells' blood relatives. They didn't have to look after either of us; no law said so.

In the dark I reached for Lena's hand.

'Whatever happens we'll stick together, you and me,' I told her.

'Too right, Nellie. I've never had a friend like you before.'

I sighed. 'So what can we do?'

'We need money – our own money so we're not a burden to anyone.'

I liked Lena's thinking. There were plenty of jobs people our age got hired to do – paper rounds or help with lambing, or mucking out horses. But I kept coming back to Mrs Lamb's offer: a sponsorship deal like that would pay for everything Lena and I could ever need. If only Mrs Lamb had chosen me.

Lena's bed creaked as she turned to face me.

'Hey, what's the story, morning glory?' she asked.

'What's your tale, nightingale?' I replied, even though it was the wrong time of day for our catchphrase.

Our fingers entwined.

'We're meant to be together, you and me,' Lena said.

I nodded in absolute agreement. 'Yup. It's you and me, no matter what.'

What we needed was a way to make it happen before the sixteenth of June.

*

That night I dreamed I was swimming through an underwater graveyard, searching for Mam's headstone. Trouble was, all the gravestones looked like hers and every single grave had yellow roses on it. There was a girl floating alongside me, wearing peculiar short trousers and swimming a funny beginner's doggy paddle. She told me they'd moved Mam's grave, but she didn't know where. So I kept searching, and the more I searched the more frustrated I grew.

'It's the Clatworthys' fault,' I told the girl. 'They take everything decent.'

Yet even then, in that awful dream, I was glad to be swimming. And gladder still, eventually, to swim home down the main street to Combe Grange, to reach out and turn the big brass door handle, and push open our front door.

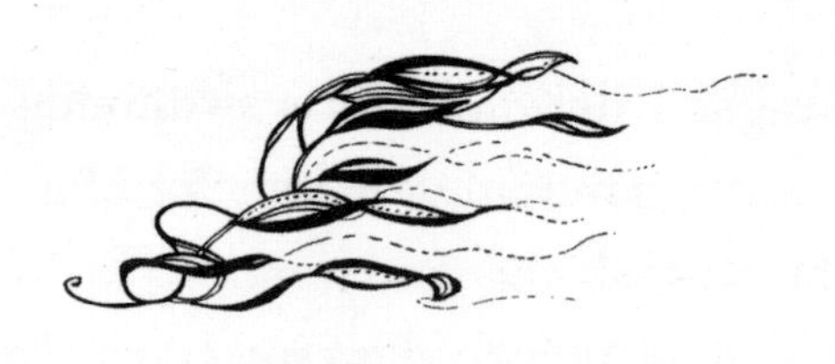

8.
SUMMER, 2032
POLLY

Now I'm out of the water, I sit for a moment to catch my breath. It's the middle of the night still, the air too warm, the sky moon-bright, and in my shorts' pocket I feel the weight of the old door handle. What the heck just happened to me? Did I imagine something lurking in the water, or did I fall asleep and dream it all? Have I drowned? Am I actually *dead*?

I pinch my arm: it definitely still hurts. The door handle feels real enough too, as does the dried mud beneath me, and the water dripping off the end of my nose. I'm here, I'm alive, and I'm very, *very* confused.

I hurry back to Jessie's in case she's out looking for me. But I find everything just as I left it: in the garden the same big dog fox is still eating leftovers under the apple trees, and in the kitchen the clock shows it's two in the morning. It's a relief, yes, but it's not logical or normal. Time doesn't just stand still.

In bed I don't for a second think I'll be able to go to sleep. When I close my eyes I see the old village again, the main street, the ford, clear as anything, as if I've just spent the evening searching it on the internet. But it's not photos I've seen, it's the real thing.

Somehow, I've been to Syndercombe.

*

Next morning, the second I wake up I'm out of bed, checking my shorts' pocket. The door handle is still there, though it's in a different position: the latch is closed. When the latch is open, like last night, I'm guessing it lets me into the past. And I become a girl called Nellie Foster.

No. That's ridiculous. I can't believe I'm even thinking this.

Joel shouts from the kitchen, asking if I want eggs. I hide the handle under my pillow. I'm not going to tell him what happened: I'm not going to tell anyone until I understand it a bit more. One thing I do know: I'm going back to the lake tonight to see if it happens again.

In the kitchen, Joel hands me a plate of scrambled eggs. He's looking happier already. Being here must be doing him good.

'Real eggs from real chickens!' he says excitedly, because at home when the shop's got no eggs we have scrambled tofu, which isn't the same thing at all.

I'm starving, I realise, as I follow Joel out into the garden. It's already too hot to be directly in the sun, so we sit cross-legged, plates on our laps, in the shade of one of Jessie's beautiful beech trees. She's out on a house call, apparently: she likes to do them early, before it gets too hot.

'They're forecasting forty-five degrees today,' Joel tells me. 'That's got to be a record, hasn't it?'

I'm not really listening. I'm thinking about Syndercombe's stone houses, the thatched rooftops, the churchyard, and how real it still feels.

Joel tuts. 'You're miles away.'

'Just hot,' I fib.

'Shame you don't like swimming,' Joel says. He takes our empty plates and gets up to go back inside. 'I might give the lake a go later.'

I'm hoping 'later' doesn't mean tonight. I've a feeling there are rules to this time-travel business, and I want to do everything exactly as I did it last night: same clothes, same time, same being alone. I'm worried it won't work otherwise. And if it doesn't then I'll never know why this has happened to me, or why I got to be Nellie Foster, or whether any of this, truly, is real.

'What else are you up to today?' I ask, following Joel into the kitchen. 'Apart from staying out of the sun.'

I'm expecting the government alerts to start early.

'Well—' By the cheeky tilt of Joel's head I guess he's about to say 'brain surgery' or 'ballroom dancing' or something equally unlikely, but he's interrupted by a knock at the front door.

As I'm the one without an armful of dishes, I go to see who it is. There's a very old woman on the doorstep.

'Hello, can I help you?' I ask.

The woman is staring up at the house, then down at a little notebook in her hand. She's wearing a tweed coat, tights *and* zip-up winter boots like it's the middle of January. It makes me break out in a sweat just looking at her.

'Is Jessie in, dear?' she asks. 'I think I had an appointment with her today, but I got a bit confused over the time.'

There's no car on the track behind her, no sign of a bike. She's walked here, then, though she must live nearby because she's leaning heavily on two walking sticks. She's probably one of Jessie's patients.

'I'm sorry, Jessie's out on visits,' I say. 'Have you tried calling her?'

The woman shuts her eyes for a second.

'Are you okay? Whoa!' I catch her by the elbow as she sways, about to faint.

'I'm sorry,' she says, shakily. 'I'm a little warm from the walk over.'

Thankfully, Joel appears, headphones on.

'What's happening?' he yells over his music.

The woman sways against me again.

'Let's get her inside.' I'm worried she's going to collapse otherwise. 'We might need a doctor.'

He takes the woman's other side, and together we help her up the steps. Through the sleeve of her thick coat I feel the tiny bones of her arm.

'Who *is* she?' Joel mouths over the top of the woman's head.

'One of Jessie's patients, I think,' I answer.

In the kitchen I fetch the woman a glass of water. No, she insists stubbornly, she doesn't need a doctor, though I manage to persuade her to take off her coat, and Joel lifts his headphones to ask her name.

'Mary,' the woman says.

Slowly, she begins to look better. She sits forward, resting her elbows on the table, cupping her face in her hands.

'Who are you two?' she asks.

'Jessie's nephew and niece,' I explain. 'I'm Polly, and this is Joel. We're here for the holidays.'

Mary peers at me. 'Yes, I see the resemblance now. What do you think of the lake? Have you been swimming yet?'

Joel's device dings in his back pocket. My brother and I both freeze. This isn't the ping-ping that the government's alert makes. This is one note, a bell chime, that means a new social media message. I've not heard it since Joel turned his phone off at Exeter station. My heart sinks, because he's obviously turned it on again. The bad internet I'd been hoping for has been upgraded since we were last here – satellites, apparently, put up in space by some mega-millionaire – so those stupid notifications are still getting through.

'Turn it off, Joel.' I can't bear to think about the film clip or the vile comments underneath.

Joel's mood changes.

'Don't tell me what to do,' he snaps.

I wince. But he does at least message Jessie before storming out into the garden. Our aunt arrives in minutes to take charge.

'Oh, Mary, it's my day to come to you, flower,' Jessie says. 'I wrote it on your calendar.'

Mary looks at her vaguely.

'I think she walked here,' I tell Jessie.

'In this heat? Oh crikey.' Jessie sighs, concerned, then says to Mary, 'Let's get you home, shall we?'

As Mary's still wobbly, Jessie asks me to go with them.

'It's at the top of the track. We'll take an arm each,' she says.

We make our way carefully up the track, turn right at the top and there, set back from the road, is a cottage attached to an old farmhouse. I can't imagine anyone lives in the farmhouse itself – half the roof has gone, and there's a tree growing out of one of the downstairs windows. Mary's cottage doesn't look much smarter: the front garden's waist-high in weeds, and the curtains are still drawn. The sign on the gate says 'Shakespeare Cottage'.

Mary notices me staring. 'Do you like the name?'

I shrug. We've done a few of his plays at school, and it seems to me that most people either love Shakespeare or hate him. Personally, I find him confusing.

'D'you understand Shakespeare?' I ask. 'Because I don't. It's like a different language. Our teacher says he made some of the words up so they sounded better.'

Mary looks startled. 'My dear, I didn't name the house after *William* Shakespeare. Its name comes from Shakespeare Beach, Dover, the popular departure point for Channel swimmers.'

I stiffen. The Channel? The *English* Channel?

Immediately, I'm back with Nellie, feeling her disappointment at not being picked to swim. It's real. A coldness in my stomach.

'You can't just set off from any old beach?' I ask.

'Not if you want to make the record books,' Mary replies, with the air of someone who knows what they're talking about. 'It all has to be done properly – at least, that's the official line.'

I'm hoping she'll keep talking, but Jessie hurries us up the path, insisting we get out of the sun. As Mary searches for her house keys, Jessie's device starts ringing. She turns away to take the call, motioning for me to help Mary inside.

'I'll only be a sec,' Jessie whispers.

After the glare of daylight, it's dark in Mary's hallway. There's a smell too, like overripe bananas or a bin that needs emptying. A couple of steps along the hall, and my foot thumps into something solid.

'Ouch!' There's stuff on the floor. Wherever I put my feet I seem to be treading on something I shouldn't be.

'Let me put the light on,' Mary says, and gropes for the switch.

The light comes on, and for a moment, I still don't know where to stand. The hall is full of black bin bags. The only way through is via a narrow gap we have to shuffle along, sideways.

The sitting room is just as messy, this time with piles of newspapers and bundles of knitting wool. Mary heads for an armchair by the window, and sits down, gladly. She's struggling to get out of her coat, so I go to help her.

'You've got a lot of stuff here,' I can't help saying.

She smiles. 'That's what happens when you've lived in the same house for a long time.'

'How long *have* you lived here?'

'Since 1952.' She answers, quick as anything. 'I was just a girl when we moved in.'

I do the maths in my head: 1952 means Mary was growing up at the same time as Nellie. The valley's not exactly big, and Syndercombe was just a village, so they must've known each other. They might even have been friends.

9.
SUMMER, 2032
POLLY

There's more I want to ask, but Jessie bustles in, hot, apologising, and immediately starts talking about tablets and blood pressure. She does a few checks on Mary, then taps the results into her screen.

'Blood pressure's up,' Jessie says. 'You feeling all right?'

Mary sighs. 'I'm not sleeping too well.'

Jessie nods sympathetically. 'That'll be the weather. We need to keep an eye on you while it's this hot, my love. Make sure you're drinking enough.'

She takes a jug to the kitchen to fill with water, leaving me and Mary alone. I seize the moment.

'Did you ever know a girl called Nellie Foster?' I ask.

Mary gives me an odd look. Then Jessie's back in the

room, shooing me away from Mary's chair, and saying her patient's had enough excitement for one day and we should leave her in peace.

On the short walk home, I ask Jessie what she knows about Mary as a girl.

'Nurses aren't supposed to talk about their patients,' she warns.

'Maybe I could talk to Mary, then? We've got this homework to do where we have to interview an old person. Mary might be up for it.'

'Talk about what?'

'Proud moments, regrets, that sort of thing.'

'I don't think so, Pol. Mary's an old lady, not coping very well with living on her own,' Jessie says.

'It'd only be a few questions. She might like a bit of company.' I realise I might too. Joel's in a huff with me; I've still not heard from Sasha. And I'm hoping Mary will be able to tell me more about Nellie.

But Jessie's firm. 'She's not well, flower. Her blood pressure's worrying me.'

'I'd only—'

Jessie stops. Turns to face me. 'Mary needs peace and quiet, okay?'

I sigh, disappointed.

'Is that doctor's orders, then?' I ask.

'Nurse's orders, actually.' She cups my cheek fondly. 'Which are far, *far* more serious.'

*

By midday, as predicted, the government alert ping-pings. We have to stay indoors until a single ping tells us the temperature's dropped. Joel slopes off to his room, still moody. I suppose he's worried about going back to school next week on top of everything else. Jessie and I close the blinds, shut the windows, and retreat to our rooms to rest. It's too hot to do much else.

'Polly?' Jessie calls a while later. 'Do old people use social media? I mean, is it a *thing*?'

What a weird question. 'Ummm . . . maybe?'

Jessie appears in my doorway, hair pinned up, wearing a sundress. She carries on talking as she moves to the kitchen. I get up and follow her, watching as she makes us both a cold drink.

'If you had a friend, say, and you lost touch over the years and wanted to track them down – this friend would be seriously old by now, like, over ninety – what's the chance you might find them online?' she asks me.

'Is this about you?' I say. 'Because you're not *that* old.'

Jessie laughs. 'You're a charmer. And no, for the record, it's not about me.'

'Mary, then?'

'Polly,' Jessie warns. 'What did I tell you?'

Begrudgingly, I suggest the sites Mum and her friends use.

'Can you put out a message, saying "X is looking for Y"?' Jessie wants to know as she hands me an apple juice so cold the glass looks like it's sweating.

'It's easier just to search the person's name.'

I get out my device.

'We could try it,' I say, thumbs hovering over my screen. 'Who's Mary looking for?'

Jessie hesitates. Takes a sip of her drink.

'I didn't say it *was* Mary,' she says.

My aunt's a rubbish liar. It *is* Mary, I'm sure of it. Could the friend she has lost touch with be Nellie? I'm dying to give the search a try.

'Let's put a name in,' I say again, but Jessie waves the idea away.

'Don't worry, flower,' she says. 'Thanks for the advice, though.' She goes back to her room.

Taking my drink into the living room, I lie on the sofa. It's frustrating the heck out of me that I can't just go back to Shakespeare Cottage and talk to Mary straight out about Nellie. And while we're on old friends, I'm beginning to realise how much I'm missing Sasha. Before, I've just felt upset and angry. I've not wanted to speak to her. But Nellie's closeness to Lena has made me remember how important good friends are. Maybe it's Sasha I need to talk to most of all.

I take a deep breath, scroll down through my device. The last message she sent me was just before we fell out at the swimming pool.

'Watcha, P. Got your water wings for later?'

Joel reckons Sasha's texts read like they've been written by someone's dad. It's true – no one texts quite like her. I'm smiling as I type in a message.

'Hi Sash. You there? Want to chat? Miss you. x'

It comes back straight away: 'Number not found'. I try again and get the same.

Has she *blocked* me?

I stare at my screen, feeling slightly sick. She's my best friend. She wouldn't.

Yeah, says a voice in my head, but best friends speak to each other, don't they? Where's she been all summer, eh?

Maybe she's changed her device, I tell myself. A lot can happen in a few weeks of not speaking.

One by one, I try all her social media accounts, and

get a similar message – 'Account doesn't exist' or 'User name not recognised'.

'Oh, come on!' I mutter. Now I can't get hold of her I want to speak to her more than ever.

Yet there's no sign of Sasha online. She's either blocked me or all her accounts have disappeared. Both possibilities are *very* weird. I'd ask Joel what I can do to find her, but his bedroom door is closed: I can hear him in there moving about, counting to three out loud, over and over. I've no idea what he's doing.

*

The rest of the day drags. Waiting to go back to Syndercombe tonight is worse than waiting for Christmas, only far, far hotter. At teatime the heat alert is still in place. I drink more water. Lie back on my bed and start browsing the internet. I type in Mary's name and address. Nothing comes up.

Next I try 'Shakespeare Beach' and get pictures and links to swimming clubs and blog posts. It's not really what I'm after. On a new search page, I type in 'Truthwater Lake'.

The first link is to the official South West Water Board's site, with information about dog walks and opening times for the café, as well as a few lines about the history of the dam. It's like reading a glossy holiday brochure, and says nothing about the people of Syndercombe who had to leave their homes behind.

Back in the search results, there's a recent newspaper article about the reservoir drying up. Some of the photos show the crumbling walls and dried mud. Others are of the old village, and it's these that make me sit up. There's the main street, thatched cottages running along either side, the pub called the White Lion, the shop with bags of coal outside. There's a picture of a man who I'm sure is Mr Blackwell, standing proudly between two huge horses. Another shows the little village school, and behind it, St Mary's church.

The pictures make me almost homesick for old Syndercombe. If I can't speak to Mary, then I have to go back there, otherwise I'll never know how Nellie's story ends, or what it means for me.

*

At last it's evening, and the temperature drops. We sit in the garden, eating the tomatoes, peppers and cucumbers Jessie grew and has made into a huge, tasty salad. I'm talking too much and eating hardly anything. I tell Joel about Sasha's online accounts.

'Weird,' he murmurs.

'Can you have a look?' I press. 'See what you think?'

He yawns. 'I'll do it later, yeah?'

Under the apple trees, a group of sparrows squabble in the dust. The dog fox comes early to drink from the water bowl Jessie puts out every night. Each time I check my device the clock has barely moved.

Yet slowly, oh so slowly, the blue of the sky fades. And just after ten, I say goodnight and hurry off to bed, and hear Joel and Jessie turning in not long afterwards: footsteps, the creak of the compost toilet's door, then a hush as the house settles down for the night. Now all I have to do is keep awake until two. The way I'm feeling, it shouldn't be hard.

In the quiet of my bedroom, I lift my pillow and take out the door handle. The brass-yellow colour of it looks grubby and worn, like a piece of ancient treasure. The handle is still in the closed position. I had wondered if it was from St Mary's church door, but now I'm pretty sure it's from the house in Syndercombe where Nellie Foster lives – or lived.

All this thinking keeps me alert. Finally, just before two o'clock, I ease myself off my bed. I pull on the same shorts and T-shirt and push the handle deep into my pocket. I even tie my hair back with the same band. I'm doing everything I did last night in the hope it works.

On tiptoe, I cross the kitchen and once I'm out in the garden, I run. The moonlight makes everything look grey. I hurry down the steps, on to the dried-up lake bed. I keep running until the ground dips and I see the lake up ahead, glistening. The nerves hit me then – it's the thought of that deep, dark water that makes my stomach clench.

'What are you doing out here?' says a voice I know.

I freeze.

Joel is at the water's edge, just as I'd dreaded. I'm annoyed and dismayed all at once.

'Couldn't sleep. Same as you, by the look of it,' I mutter.

Joel faces me, big-eyed and apologetic.

'Sorry, Pol,' he says. 'I was horrible to you today.'

I stare at him. Past him.

'S'all right.' Really, all I'm thinking is, *You have to tell me this NOW?*

'I've been on one, haven't I?' He prods the water with his toe. 'I want to tell you about it, if that's okay?'

But I feel a click against my hip. The handle in my pocket is turning. I'm desperate for Joel to go back to bed, or disappear, or just not be standing in front of me at this precise moment. He'll try and stop me going in the lake, I know he will, and the seconds are ticking away. If I don't swim now I'm afraid it won't work at all.

'Sorry, but can we have this conversation later?' I say, and stride into the water with such determination, Joel steps aside in surprise.

'Don't go too far in,' he warns.

'Yeah, okay,' I call over my shoulder. 'I'm a rubbish swimmer. You've told me.'

'Just be careful,' Joel cries. 'Hey! Are you listening?'

Not any more.

The water rises up around me. When I'm chest deep I take the handle out again to check – sure enough, it's in the open position. Not wanting to miss another moment, I start to swim. And when I reach the middle, I dive down and down until the gravestones appear, and it's daytime.

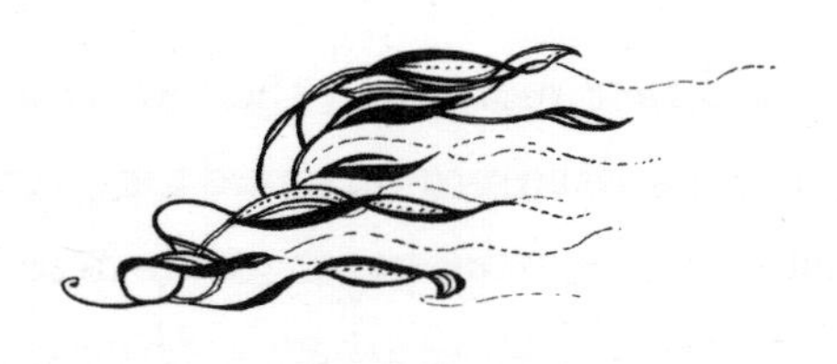

10.
SPRING, 1952
NELLIE

When I woke the next morning my hair was damp again, my nightgown sticking wetly to my chest.

'What's the story—' Lena stopped, mid-catchphrase. 'Oh, Nell, you've had a fever!'

She'd often had horrid night sweats like it when she'd been ill.

'I'm all right,' I said, brushing off her concern and getting out of bed.

Yet the graveyard dream stayed with me all day, leaving me wrung out and limp, as if I really had been swimming in my sleep. I couldn't concentrate in lessons. I barely spoke to anyone in the playground. Ma Blackwell's plan to send Lena back to London, and me to the orphanage – possibly – had shaken me to my bones. I couldn't bear it. We needed our own plan, Lena and me. And I'd a feeling it'd take more than the money a paper round could provide to ensure we stayed together.

That same day work began on the reservoir. Despite Mr Clatworthy's promise that we'd have time to get used to the idea, life in our little village started changing at a galloping pace. First it was the trucks arriving, brutish and noisy, that churned up mud, frightened the livestock and sent us clambering into hedges to avoid being crushed on our daily walk to school.

The trucks brought the workers, some with clipboards, most with shovels, pickaxes and leathery, lined faces, who set up camp just outside the village. Their tools tip-tapped and their machinery rumbled all day long. Yet we only ever saw the men themselves if they came to the shop for cigarettes or a pint at the White Lion, or at night when their tents lit up like paper lanterns on the hillside.

Almost as soon as the workers arrived, the locals began to leave. Among the first to go were the six tuberculosis patients from the huts in the Blackwells' orchard – three went home to their families, the other three to a sanatorium near the sea. It happened just before school one morning: Lena and I watched from an upstairs window as nurses helped the sickest patients into a waiting ambulance.

'They'd better not try taking *me* away!' Lena cried, genuinely worried at the possibility. 'I'm not ill any more!'

Sometimes, when the mornings were cold, she'd rub her breastbone with her fist and say her chest felt tight. Yet really, we all knew she'd recovered from the TB. In its own cruel way, that was part of the problem.

'Ma Blackwell wouldn't dare put *you* in an ambulance!' I assured her, though putting her on a train home to London was a different matter entirely, and if we didn't think up an alternative, it would be happening.

*

Saturday at the lido was the first proper chance Lena and I had to consider what we were going to do. June was only a few months away. Yet, though we'd been on tenterhooks all week, Ma Blackwell hadn't mentioned anyone leaving again. Like everyone else in Syndercombe, the Blackwells were taken up with the workmen arriving and the changes already under way. People talked of little else.

As usual, we caught the one o'clock bus into Minehead, wearing our swimsuits under our clothes so we didn't waste precious time getting changed. I'd braced myself for seeing Nate Clatworthy again. Though

I wasn't exactly looking forward to hearing about his training regime with Mrs Lamb, a bigger part of me was dying to know everything. So I was quite disappointed when Captain Farley informed us, at the start of the session, that Nate would no longer be attending our club.

'He'd barely started, anyway,' Bob pointed out.

'Huh! He still walked off with the prize though, didn't he, eh?' muttered Jim.

'Not fair,' Maudie agreed.

'It is simply a matter of temperature,' the captain told us firmly. 'Even our pool is too warm for a would-be Channel swimmer. From now on young Clatworthy will be training outside in open water, so there we are.'

'Yes, but where?' I asked.

The captain, who seemed to think the conversation finished and was already directing the others into the pool, looked irritated. '*Where?*'

'Where's he swimming, sir? Is it Mrs Lamb who's training him?'

The captain rolled his eyes. 'Oh, get in the water, Nellie, for heaven's sake! Enough about Master Clatworthy! Think about your own swimming, why don't you?'

But that was exactly it – I *was* thinking about my own swimming, because whatever Nate Clatworthy was doing, I wanted to be doing it too. I was even willing to watch him train, to talk to him about his new regime. How else would I learn how to be a Channel swimmer?

That afternoon, the pool felt like tepid bathwater. I swam badly. My legs wouldn't kick properly; my arms were too heavy. Countless times Captain Farley told me to buck up and concentrate. At one point, even Maudie asked me if I was all right. I said I was, thank you, but all I could think about was Nate, and the special training he was doing, and how I'd give anything to have that chance.

Afterwards, Lena and I went to the nearest tearoom for our usual post-swimming currant buns. We bought an extra bun to take home for Perry and Sage, then found a seat near the window and shed our coats.

'So,' I said, my mouth full of bun. 'What are we going to do to earn money?'

'For the Blackwells?' Lena asked, calmly pouring our tea.

'For our future, Lena! We need a – oh!'

Seeing Captain Farley enter the tearoom, I stopped, mid-rant. He made a beeline for our table, which gave me just enough time to swallow my mouthful.

'Did I forget my towel?' Lena asked when he reached us, because she was often leaving things behind.

'What? No.' The captain turned to me, dropping his voice. 'The gravel pits, Nellie, up at Marley's Head. That's where you'll find the boy, if you're interested.'

Somehow, he knew I would be.

I stood up immediately, reaching for my coat. 'Thank you, Captain Farley.'

'We haven't finished our tea,' Lena wailed.

But this couldn't wait.

*

A short while later we were standing in the road at Marley's Head, the bus disappearing round the bend.

'Now where?' Lena asked.

The afternoon light was beginning to fade, and Marley's Head was a desolate sort of place, high up and bleak. It was where two smaller rivers merged before tumbling through our valley, and the spot the water board had chosen to reroute their flow. The evidence of it – razed hedges, trenches, fields turned to mud – was already in plain sight, and quite a shock. I had to remind myself that we were here for something far more exciting.

The gravel pits were down a lane that hardly anyone ever used.

'This way,' I said, beckoning to Lena. 'Come on, slowcoach!'

A few yards along the lane we reached a gateway set back in the hedge. The gate itself, hanging wonkily on its hinges, opened on to a narrow track that, unless you knew otherwise, appeared to be a dead end. The track led to an old gravel pit, about the size of four swimming pools and filled with very deep, very cold water. It was the sort of place where, if a person went missing, the police would search for a body. It was also a brilliant spot for open-water swimming.

All along the track, the flattened grass and muddy footprints were a sure sign that someone was already here.

'Nate?' Lena asked, pointing at a large shoe print.

'Got to be. Crikey, he's got big feet!'

Lena giggled. 'Flippers, more like!'

The gravel pit was just around the corner. The path stopped high above it, giving us the most wonderful view of the water below.

'Looks like a lake on the moon,' remarked Lena, and I knew what she meant.

The pit was bordered on all sides by steep, bare, shingle slopes which ran right down to the water's edge. The water, cloudy and iron grey, looked as cold as the Arctic Ocean. The only splash of colour was an abandoned yellow towel, spread out halfway up the slope. Next to it lay a boy's bicycle. Out in the water, swimming a slow front crawl, was Nate Clatworthy. I was expecting a focused training session like the ones we had at the pool but this, unfortunately, looked more like a nice afternoon dip.

'Where's Mrs Lamb?' I wondered.

'Gone back to America, I suppose,' Lena replied.

'Well, he's a silly beggar, swimming out here all by himself,' I muttered. It was our club's golden rule to never go into open water on your own.

'Bet it's cold in there,' Lena said with a shiver.

'That *is* the point.'

It was cold where we were too, high up above the water: the wind in our faces had a bite to it, and against our legs, the chill of the evening rose from the ground. Once we'd found a more sheltered spot, we sat, hugging our knees and watching.

I didn't take my eyes off Nate as he swam. Up and back, up and back: he travelled the length of the lake in his unfussy style. It *would* be cold in that water: possibly less than fifty degrees Fahrenheit at this time of year. Anyone who could cope with that sort of cold was, I had to admit, doing well. The old feeling of envy stirred in me as I watched. I'd so wanted to be Mrs Lamb's Channel swimmer, and seeing Nate do what I'd give my back teeth for felt both thrilling and like punching a bruise.

Suddenly, he stopped swimming. Something seemed to be wrong. He was reaching under the water to his leg or foot and struggling to stay afloat.

Lena stiffened beside me. 'D'you suppose he's all right?'

I was on my feet that instant, running, sliding, slipping down the slope, Lena right behind me. By the time we reached the water's edge, there was no sign of Nate. He'd vanished under the surface.

'I knew that boy was trouble,' I hissed, yanking off my coat.

Lena stared at me. 'You're going *in*? In your clothes?'

I stepped out of my skirt and wriggled free of my sweater, till I was down to my shirt and underwear. As much as I hated Nate Clatworthy, we couldn't leave him to drown.

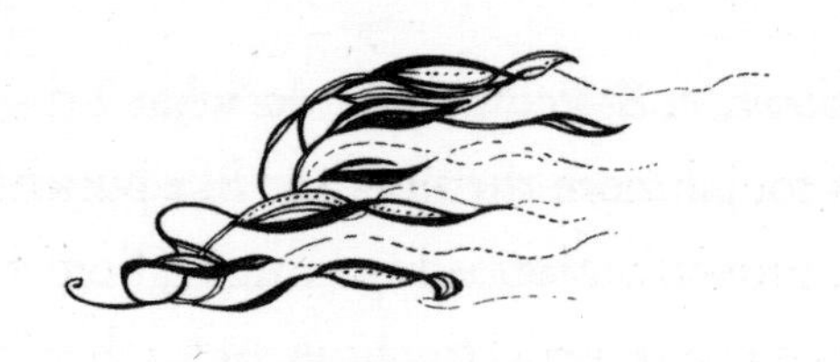

11.
SPRING, 1952
NELLIE

Nate surfaced again, spluttering and panicking. As I swam towards him, I tried to remember how to rescue a drowning person. We'd practised it at swimming club, so I knew that I had to get behind him and hook my arms under his armpits. It'd been easy enough in a pool, but the water was so cold my whole body felt heavy. And Nate, in his panic, wouldn't keep still. He kept slipping under. Bobbing up. Slipping under. If this rescue was going to work, I had to stay calm.

'Okay, Nate,' I said, manoeuvring myself behind him. 'I'm going to swim you back to shore.'

It was as if he hadn't heard me. He kept trying to turn round, lashing out so I couldn't get hold of him. Our legs kicked against each other's. Water stung my eyes. There was a danger of us both going under at this rate.

'You have to keep still,' I warned.

A couple more attempts and finally I managed to grab him properly. Nate stopped struggling. The top of his head was now beneath my chin.

'That's good,' I told him.

Kicking furiously, I steered us towards the shore. It didn't look far – a length of the pool, at most. But the cold was brutal. I couldn't feel my fingers. Nate had gone from wriggling like a ferret in a sack to being limp and very quiet. He was losing consciousness, I quickly realised, and that wasn't a good sign.

'Hey!' Lena called from the water's edge.

Something landed beside me with a slap. Lena yelled 'grab it' or 'hold it', I couldn't catch the exact words. My free arm reached out to find a tree branch in the water. On the other end of it, some twenty feet away, was Lena. She'd waded into the shallows, skirt tucked into her knickers, and was shouting like the bossiest games mistress in existence.

'I'll pull you in if you grab on!' she cried.

I grasped the branch, my other arm around Nate, as Lena pulled. Moments later, we were back in water shallow enough to stand up in. Nate's legs couldn't hold him, so Lena took one side, I took the other, and together we heaved him on to land. He was shivering so hard his whole body shook. What worried me most was how he kept closing his eyes.

'Nate! Don't go to sleep!' I cried, then said to Lena, 'Get his towel, can you – and his clothes!'

We wrapped the towel around him, then his jumper, his coat, his hat and scarf, and made him sit up. He kept shaking. I was shivering too, my hands and teeth juddering.

'Can you w-w-w-w-walk?' I asked him.

Nate blinked drowsily. 'What d'you say?'

'We need to g-g-g-get you moving, to w-w-w-warm you up.' But when I tried to pull him to his feet he was a dead weight. Even between us, Lena and I couldn't move him again.

'It's no good. We'll have to fetch help,' said Lena.

Yet there was, I remembered, another way to warm up, and it involved us huddling together. Not that I fancied putting my arms around Nate Clatworthy again, but I fancied fetching his father even less.

Quickly, I pulled on my dry skirt and sweater. Then, crouching beside Nate, I beckoned for Lena to do the same.

'We need to hug him. You and me together. It's the best way to get his body temperature up.'

Lena hesitated. 'Promise me you're not joking?'

'Cross-my-heart, swear-on-my-life promise,' I assured her.

So I wrapped my arms around Nate Clatworthy, Lena did the same, and we hugged each other warm.

*

Afterwards, all I wanted was hot tea and a fried egg sandwich – if the hens had laid today, that was, for all the upheaval had upset their routines too. But Nate took longer than I did to recover enough for the walk home. Fully dressed, he was still shivering. We made him keep moving until the colour came back to his cheeks. And even then I got the distinct impression he wasn't in any hurry to leave. He'd found a bar of Fruit & Nut in his coat pocket, and suggested sitting in the afternoon sun and sharing his chocolate.

I don't mind admitting it was the chocolate that persuaded me. The bar was bigger than the ones Ma Blackwell hid on the kitchen shelf: Lena couldn't take her eyes off it, either. So we climbed back up the slope into the sunshine which, thankfully, had some much-needed warmth to it.

'Funny, it's as if I already know you both,' Nate remarked, handing round the Fruit & Nut. 'Yet we've not been *properly* introduced, have we?'

'Hard to when you were being sick in a hedge or drowning because of cramp,' Lena reminded him.

'It's not happened before, you know, the cramp,' Nate said. He swallowed his chocolate quickly, I noticed, not like Lena and me, who sucked ours slowly like boiled sweets.

'Still, you shouldn't train on your own. It's dangerous,' I pointed out. 'Hasn't Captain Farley told you that?'

'No.'

'He *is* training you, though, now Mrs Lamb's gone?'

'Officially, yes. He'll get more involved nearer the swim itself.' Nate smiled sheepishly. 'I don't believe he thinks much of me, actually.'

'There's a surprise,' Lena muttered.

'I meant, as a swimmer,' Nate said, reddening. 'But you're right. I wouldn't expect him to like me: I'm a Clatworthy, after all.'

He looked so downcast that for a moment I felt sorry for him. Maybe it wasn't quite fair to hold Nate personally responsible for what his father and the water board were doing.

'It does seem a terrible shame for Syndercombe to end up like the lost city of Atlantis,' said Nate.

I blinked. 'The *what*?'

'Don't worry, that's his posh education talking,' Lena whispered to me. But I made a mental note to look up 'Atlantis' in our school encyclopaedia on Monday morning.

'What I mean,' Nate tried again, 'is that if this was my home I'd be heartbroken about what's happening.'

'But it's not *your* home,' I pointed out, the old anger rising up in me again. 'It's ours. I was born here.'

Lena put a reassuring arm around my shoulders.

'It's not just about the dam,' she explained to Nate. 'You took Nellie's place at the swimming club. Captain Farley said if it wasn't for you she'd have been picked to train with Mrs Lamb—'

'Lena, don't tell him that!' I cried, squirming with embarrassment.

'Don't flip your lid! It's true!' she insisted.

Nate looked at me, stunned. 'You really *wanted* to swim the Channel?'

'Why, don't you?'

'Do I look like I'm enjoying it?' he said, and laughed.

His reaction threw me: so he *wasn't* thrilled that Mrs Lamb picked him? This *wasn't* a dream-come-true moment?

'Why are you doing it, then?' I wanted to know.

'Because my father told me to.'

'Oh.' I nodded. '*Him.*'

'Now look here, it's complicated, all right?' Nate replied, suddenly defensive. 'I ran away from school last term, and he's not yet forgiven me for it.'

Mrs Lee had already told us that before coming here, Nate had gone to an expensive boarding school in Surrey. This wasn't unusual for boys of his sort: the running-away part, though, sounded rebellious and brave and made him go up in my estimation. Lena was also looking at him with new interest.

'What happened?' I asked, because most of us Syndercombe kids loved school.

Miss Setherton was a firm but fair teacher, and though we sometimes laughed at Tom and Bob for being goofs, it was all done in good heart.

Nate grimaced. 'I suppose you'd call them bullies. You know the sort – can't stand anyone who's different.'

'*Different?* You?' Lena looked surprised. 'In what way, exactly?'

She had a point. I'd been with Lena when people stared at her because she wasn't white, or spoke to her slowly as if she didn't understand English. Whereas Nate was from a wealthy British family, at a school full of boys just like him. It was hard to see why he wouldn't fit in.

Nate reddened again. 'Let's just say I'm not a natural at studying, especially the reading and writing part.'

'Oh?' I frowned. He sounded properly clever to me.

'It's the words,' he said. 'They jump about on the page, and muddle my head, and some boys in my class think it's great sport to make fun of me.'

'Sounds tough,' Lena murmured.

'You're a decent swimmer, though,' I reminded him.

'Maybe. Joining the club was Father's idea. He said if I couldn't cope with schoolwork then I had to succeed at sport to prove I wasn't an awful embarrassment to the family.'

Again, I felt a pang of pity for Nate. The Blackwells might not be my real parents, but they never made me feel I wasn't good enough.

'For what it's worth, I'm rubbish at spelling,' I admitted.

'I'm useless at algebra,' said Lena. Really she was good at maths, but it was nice of her to pretend.

'You're doing this to please your family, then?' I asked.

He shrugged. 'It's that or be sent back to school before the end of term.'

It didn't seem a strong enough reason, not to me. Swimming the English Channel was a huge challenge. He should want to do it from the ends of his hair to the tips of his toes. It should be all he was thinking about.

It should be keeping him awake at night.

'What do your parents think of your swimming, Nellie?' Nate asked.

The question took me by surprise. 'Umm . . . they're both dead so I couldn't say.'

'We live with the Blackwells,' Lena explained.

'*Did* live with the Blackwells, if we don't sort something out soon,' I reminded her.

Nate looked confused.

'I'll explain over a fried egg sandwich,' I told him, getting to my feet and pulling Lena up as I did so.

'She makes a good one,' Lena added. 'Runny yolk, crispy edges. Lots of salt.'

I nodded at Lena. 'Well, she makes amazing scrambled eggs with chillies.'

Nate didn't move.

'You're inviting me to *your* house?' he asked, somewhat amazed.

'Sure, why not? Unless your dad told you not to mix with us locals.'

'No, no! Not at all!' Nate stood up, grinning from ear to ear. 'I'd love to. I mean, thank you, that's jolly marvellous! I accept!'

I'd a feeling it was a long time since anyone had invited Nate Clatworthy to tea.

*

Back at Combe Grange we made fried-egg sandwiches. I admit, I was glad the Blackwells weren't in, so I didn't have to explain Nate Clatworthy's presence in their kitchen. I was still getting used to the idea myself. It wasn't that I'd suddenly forgotten what his father was here to do, more that something in me had softened. Maybe it was the swim itself, the cold of it, the challenge. Or maybe it was talking to Nate, and realising that we all had disappointments and secrets, and sharing them made us feel a bit more connected, somehow.

'You could train with him,' Lena whispered, after we'd eaten and were clearing away the dishes.

All through tea I'd thought of little else. Captain Farley, I was pretty certain, had told me where Nate was training because he knew I'd be curious. And the truth was, Nate and I could learn a lot from each other if we became training buddies. Besides, after today's performance at the gravel pits, Nate would hardly need reminding that it wasn't safe to swim alone.

When I suggested it, he agreed very readily.

'I say, Nellie! That would be top! Perhaps we could even swap places and *you* do the Channel swim.'

I laughed. He had to be joking, surely.

'Nice idea,' I replied. 'But that'd never work.'

Lena's eyebrows shot up. '*Wouldn't* it?'

'Probably not,' Nate admitted. 'It's all very official. Done through the Channel Swimming Association, so you have to register your name, and have a pilot travelling with you. Mrs Lamb explained it all.'

'And there's the sponsorship deal with the chewing gum man,' I pointed out.

Nate nodded. 'I suppose that scuppers that, then.'

'Still, no harm in dreaming,' said Lena.

'No harm at all,' I agreed, and felt myself smiling.

It wasn't that we had a plan yet, Lena and I. But I felt hopeful that one was on the way.

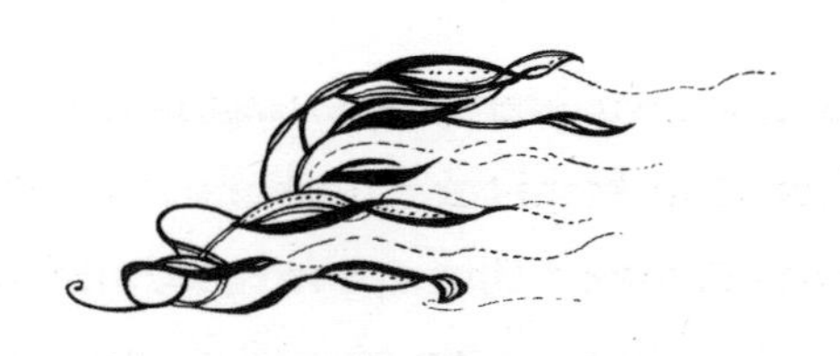

12.
SPRING, 1952
NELLIE

We agreed to train on Tuesdays, Thursdays and Saturdays. On the weekdays it meant getting up before school when the water was at its coldest, and the sky barely light.

'Sometimes I think you'd been better off born a fish,' Ma Blackwell remarked when I told her. 'You stay safe, now.'

'That's why we're training together,' I assured her.

It was no surprise that she disapproved of Nate. Mr Clatworthy wasn't popular in our village for obvious reasons, not least because the water board's compensation amounts for people's property had turned out to be a whole lot less than he'd first suggested. Money was more of a problem now than ever.

'Nate's not like his dad,' I tried to explain.

Ma Blackwell remained unconvinced. 'The apple doesn't fall far from the tree, Nellie.'

Mostly, though, she seemed glad to have Lena and me out from under her feet. And now we no longer went to swimming club, that saved a few pence too. On our last day there, Maudie sulked at our news and Captain Farley rewarded me with an awkward pat on the shoulder.

'Bravo, young Nell,' he boomed when I told him. 'That *is* an honourable gesture.'

'I'm mostly doing it to improve my own swimming, sir,' I pointed out, in case he thought I'd become some sort of saint.

*

Our first week at the gravel pits mostly involved getting used to the freezing water. The hardest part of swimming the English Channel was coping with the cold, and in June the sea would be little more than fifty-four degrees Fahrenheit. Temperatures this low could cause hypothermia or disorientate a swimmer into going miles off course. Swimming at the lido in unheated water had given me a head start, certainly, but we needed to build up our resilience.

From this point on, Nate and I agreed to avoid hot baths, hot-water bottles, piping-hot drinks, and to sleep without blankets with our bedroom windows wide open. Often I'd lie awake listening to the night-time noises – the fox cries, the owl screams, the new-born lambs bleating. Soon our whole valley would be gone: it was another lesson in resilience.

By the second week of training, things started to slip. Nate arrived late or without his proper kit, and I began to wonder for whose benefit I was doing this.

'You're the better swimmer, Nell,' Lena would grumble. 'I wish you could swap places. *You* should be the first child to swim the English Channel, not him.'

But Mrs Lamb had made her choice, and she'd picked Nate. All I could do was hope for a chance of my own in the future, though that possibility seemed a very long way off.

Then, early one Saturday morning, Lena made her brilliant mistake.

We'd agreed to meet at the usual time, and Nate was late. It was a bitter morning, a thick frost still whitening the gorse bushes. Impatient to get in the water, I decided to start without him, peeling off my clothes to my costume underneath. It was an old-fashioned thing Ma Blackwell had dug out for me ages ago – black, knitted, with thick shoulder straps and a tendency to go saggy in the water.

'Bet she wore that when she was a girl!' Lena sniggered the first time she saw me in it.

The truth was costume fashions hadn't changed much and Nate's, though considerably newer and less saggy, was the same tunic-shaped, torso-covering type as mine. It was at this point he appeared, whizzing down the slope on his bike.

'Sorry!' he said, flinging his bike aside. The smell of bacon and toast wafted from his clothes as he unbuttoned his coat.

'You'd better not have eaten too much breakfast,' I warned.

He smiled and handed me something orange and rubbery. It was a swim cap like his own.

'For you,' he said.

It was typical Nate, I was learning. He had an infuriating knack for doing something kind just when you wanted to be cross with him.

Reluctantly I took the cap. 'Thanks.'

'You'll be easier to spot in the water, wearing that,' Lena said approvingly. It was her job to time us, and she was already setting her watch. 'Thirty minutes, okay?'

'Forty-five,' I countered.

Nate groaned.

Finally, we were ready. It was one of those rare mornings where the air was colder than the water. After the first dip, the first gasp, I quickly felt warmer. Remembering to breathe slowly, I started swimming.

Our usual route was to do laps of the gravel pit. Sometimes we'd swim side by side, but often I'd edge ahead, and Nate would tuck in behind. It suited us to swim this way: he liked it that I set the pace, and I enjoyed seeing nothing but water ahead of me, because then I could almost imagine I was swimming in the open sea.

By the time Lena gave us a sign that we'd five minutes left, my shoulders ached with cold. I tried to block it out by concentrating on my rhythm.

Take a breath, lift my left arm, kick, kick. Take a breath, lift my right arm, kick, kick.

My mind drifted to breakfast, warm towels, and I reached the far side sooner than I realised. Turning straight round again, I swam back to Lena. She gave me an excited thumbs up as I neared the shore. Not stopping to touch the bottom, I turned again. I kept focused. The far side of the lake, the great sheer rock wall of it, rose up in front of me.

The cold was digging its claws in.

Breathe, arm, kick, kick.

My feet had gone numb. My shoulders creaked. I'd swum too fast, I knew I had, and being tired made the cold much harder to take. Some way behind me, Nate was also struggling.

'I can't . . .' he gasped. 'I . . . can't.'

I doubled back on myself so we'd swim the final yards together. He hit the shore just before I did, collapsing on his hands and knees. Lena came rushing over to help.

'Blimey, Nellie! Are you okay? What h—?' As she crouched down next to him, she realised her mistake. 'Oops! Sorry – I mean *Nate*, don't I?'

Nate wobbled to his feet. 'Thought you said the caps made us easier to spot in the water.'

'It's the costumes, the caps, and you're in and out so quickly,' Lena tried to explain. 'But I should've realised Nellie wouldn't collapse like that.'

'You're right,' Nate replied grimly. 'She wouldn't.'

We dressed quickly and in heavy silence. Just a week ago, when we'd started training, we'd been eager and hopeful. But something had changed. Yes, the cold had been particularly sharp this morning, but what bothered me was Nate himself.

'Next time eat a smaller breakfast,' I advised him.

'That's not the only problem, though, is it?' he said.

His shoulders slumped.

'Actually, I've not been completely honest. You see, it's not only words that muddle me – it's schedules and timetables, and remembering where I'm supposed to be and when.'

'Oh.' Though I didn't quite understand, I saw how frustrated he was – so much so there were tears in his eyes.

'As for the swimming, well, I'm fooling myself, aren't I? It's obvious I'm not good enough.'

'We could train on Wednesdays too, if you want?' I suggested.

'That's decent of you.' Nate smiled weakly. 'But I've pretty much decided. It's best for everyone if I go back to school and finish the year properly.'

I stared at him in surprise. 'Do you *want* to do that?'

'Of course not!' He said it with such force I realised then that *this* was what he wanted – not the swim, not the glory of being the first child across the Channel. What he wanted more than anything was not to go back to the school where bullies had made his life a misery.

We trudged up the slope.

'I am sorry,' Lena said. 'I didn't mean to offend anyone.

It's just you *did* look so alike for a moment.'

Nate tried to make a joke of it. 'Perhaps you need your eyes testing, old girl?'

I stopped as the idea dawned on me.

'What date is your swim, Nate?' I asked.

'They're hoping for June: it's not yet been confirmed.'

Lena and me shared a look: June was also the month of the village deadline.

'And the time?' I asked.

'The middle of the night.' Nate stopped. 'Why are you asking?'

'Well.' I paused: my heart was racing. 'If Lena made a mistake with our costumes and caps, who's to say it couldn't happen again? Especially in the heat of the moment, when you're about to start your swim, in the dark, with the pressure on.'

A slow, mischievous smile spread over Lena's face. She understood my meaning exactly. Nate, though, had gone very quiet.

I felt suddenly wrong-footed. Deep down, I suspected part of Nate *did* want to do the swim, and get his name in the history books. Plus, was doing it to please his dad such a terrible thing? If I ever swam the Channel I'd do it for Lena.

'Sorry,' I said, back-pedalling. 'I just thought—'

'We could swap places, like I suggested the other day?' Nate asked.

'Well . . .' I picked a loose thread on my coat sleeve. 'We could pretend to train you, only train *me* instead.'

'Which would keep you here in Syndercombe, wouldn't it?' Lena chipped in. 'So you wouldn't have to go back to school.'

Nate's eyes went dinner-plate wide. 'By jingo! If we could make it work that would be—'

'The answer to all our prayers?' suggested Lena.

'Would it, though?' Suddenly, I wasn't sure. 'What about afterwards when they realise we've swapped? Nate's dad'll go spare!'

'It won't matter by then,' Nate replied. 'My prep school finishes at the end of June. When the term begins again in September I'll be starting at senior school, hopefully without the bullies.'

I trembled with excitement: *could* it work?

'What about the Channel Swimming people?' I pressed. 'You said everything had to be done officially.'

'We'll find a way,' Lena assured me. 'We have to, Nellie, don't we?'

I nodded so fast I felt dizzy. This wasn't just about doing the swim or helping Nate out of a fix. It was about our future, mine and Lena's. The sponsorship money would keep us both in dinners and clothes and swimming lessons for years. Ma Blackwell wouldn't have to send Lena home or me to the orphanage. She'd never have to worry about money again.

But could us swapping places really work? There'd be officials everywhere – the pilot, Captain Farley, Mrs Lamb and someone from the chewing gum company. Not to mention all the newspapers who'd want to capture the big event.

And what would happen at the end when it was me, not Nate, walking up the beach in France? What if the sponsors didn't pay up?

Nate brushed it off. 'Ah, you'll be so famous every news reporter will want your story.'

'And if the swim *is* allowed,' Lena reminded me. 'And the sponsors do pay you the money—'

'It'll be blooming brilliant!' I admitted.

Though the idea we might get away with it was the wildest thing I'd ever heard.

*

Yet Lena wasn't the only one to mistake me for Nate, because a few days later it happened again. Without warning, Captain Farley appeared at the gravel pits to watch us train. I was the only one in the water at the time, cap and costume on, swimming my laps. It was pure luck that Lena and Nate were on the far side of the gravel pit, and the weather so raw that they were almost hidden under thick coats and an old horse blanket.

The captain stayed for what felt like ages. I tried to swim as normal, concentrating on my breathing and my stroke. But I was nervous – and grew more so when I saw he'd moved closer to where the others were sitting. I hoped Lena had a good excuse ready for why it was me, not Nate, in the water. Or that Nate would charm his way out of the situation. We couldn't have the captain getting suspicious: if he did, the swap idea would be over before it'd properly begun.

I was expecting the worst, when the captain called out: 'Bravo, young man! You've come on leaps and bounds these past weeks!'

My stroke slowed as I realised *he* didn't recognise me, either. The orange cap, the black costume, the distance across the water, all convinced him that I was Nate. He hadn't even recognised the difference in our swimming styles. Thrilled, I glanced at Lena, who, from under the shelter of the horse blanket, was giving me a thumbs up. The mistake we were pinning our hopes on had worked – again!

Once the captain had finally gone and I exited the water, I felt deliriously happy.

This time it was Nate's turn to be cautious.

'We've got to get you on to the pilot's boat first, old bean, to give you an official reason to be there,' he said.

I nodded to show I'd understood, that I was ready, whatever it took.

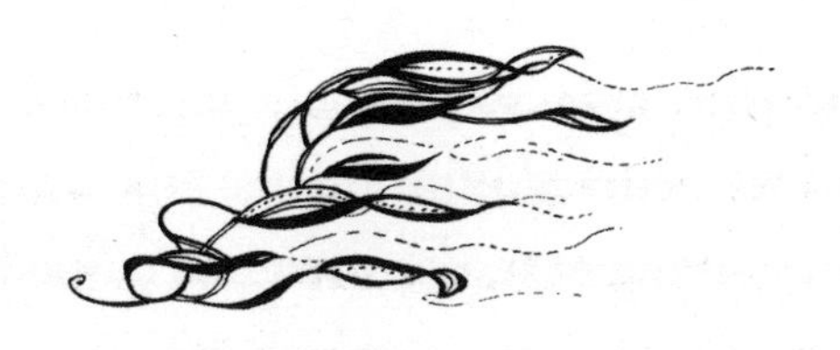

13.
SPRING, 1952
NELLIE

Meanwhile, work on the reservoir continued at great speed. Every day now our once-peaceful village was choked with trucks, vans and the noise and fumes they brought with them.

'D'you think people actually know,' I asked Lena, 'what has to happen for there to be fresh water in their taps?'

'I suppose it's convenient, but there's a price to pay, isn't there?'

'Yeah, there is – Syndercombe.'

Yet amazingly, many of the locals had already accepted what was happening, calling it progress and 'for the greater good' and saying how a country that had beaten Hitler deserved the very best for its growing towns and cities. I suspected this was something Mr

Clatworthy had told people – and told them again – until they believed him. Village talk was full of what was happening next, not what had been. All eyes were on the future.

In a way, I could understand it: we too, were taking a huge, exciting step into the unknown with the Channel swim swap, which, if it worked out, would change our lives for ever. Yet I also knew that saying goodbye to Syndercombe was going to break my heart.

Already in the lower valley the dam wall was visible over the treetops. It'd gone up so quickly my brain couldn't make sense of seeing so much concrete against the bright, budding oaks and elms. The fact that spring had arrived and the valley looked so beautiful made it harder. I'd been born here. My mam had died here. It felt wrong to move her from the churchyard to the new cemetery in town. Yet that day was fast approaching, which made me all the more determined not to lose Lena as well. Our wildly unlikely plan simply *had* to work. For it to stand a chance, though, I'd need to be on board the pilot boat: the question was how to make it happen.

*

Quite by chance, a peach of an opportunity came along one day after school. We'd taken the horses out for a ride: with little work for them to do nowadays, they were excitable and fresh, so we went for a canter over the fields. Back in the village, we stopped at the post office because we'd heard Mrs Lee had sugar mice in stock and it was first come first served. As Lena went in to buy some, I waited outside with the horses.

'What do you think about leaving here, boy?' I asked Perry, clapping his neck. 'D'you fancy going somewhere new?'

Though there'd still been no word on the Blackwells' plans, I was certain they'd be moving to another farm. Mr Blackwell wouldn't be parted from his beloved horses. Him without Perry and Sage was like me without Lena, the sun without the stars. It wouldn't – couldn't – happen.

Just as Lena exited the shop with an impressively large bag of sweets, Mrs Lee called her back.

'You girls don't have a minute to deliver this, do you?' She was holding a telegram. 'Only my usual boy's got chickenpox.'

'Who's it for?' Lena asked, craning her neck to see the address.

'The captain. At Hadfield Hall. You'll have to be

quick to catch him, he's moving out this afternoon.'

All week we'd seen removal vans going to and from the hall, carrying carpets, oil paintings, crates of straw-packed valuables.

'Doesn't he have children to give it to?' Lena had asked, when Ma Blackwell told us what the captain couldn't fit into his new house was being sold at auction.

'There's never been a wife or a child.' Though she'd said it with a nervous cough which made me wonder if she wasn't telling us everything.

I reached for the telegram.

'We'll do it, Mrs Lee,' I agreed.

Hadfield Hall had always intrigued me. It was built in Elizabethan times as a hunting lodge, and rumour had it Queen Elizabeth I had stayed there. The house had very tall, twisting red-brick chimneys: the new reservoir, so Ma Blackwell had said, had to be especially deep to cover them. There was another reason too. Hadfield Hall was where Mam had worked, and I'd not been back since she died. This would be my final chance to visit.

Perry set off at a raking trot, Sage having to canter to keep up.

'Slow down or I'll drop the sugar mice!' yelled Lena.

Easing into a walk, we turned left before the ford, and followed the lane uphill slightly. A hundred yards or so along it, we came to a pair of iron gates that today were almost lost under the ivy and knotweed. The drive itself looked neglected too, and ended in a courtyard so familiar I almost burst into tears.

There was the old horse trough and beside it the smaller, lower one for the captain's dogs to drink from. Various herbs still grew in pots outside the kitchen door, and the boot jack, caked in fresh mud, hadn't moved from its spot by the tack room. I almost expected Mam to appear, duster in hand.

We slid down from the horses, knocked on the back door, and waited. From inside came the sound of furniture being moved. Someone shouted instructions. A door slammed.

'I don't think they heard you,' I said, when no one appeared.

Lena tucked the telegram under her arm, flicked her braid over her shoulder, and this time used both fists to pound the door.

Still no one came.

'Wonder what's in this telegram?' Lena muttered, flipping it open.

'Lena!' I gasped, shocked and impressed. 'You can't just open—'

The look on her face shut me up.

'What is it?' I cried. 'What does it say?'

She thrust the message at me to read.

'ONLY ONE SWIMMER PLACE AVAILABLE FOR JUNE *stop* PROVIDE NC DETAILS BY RETURN TO SECURE DATE FOR SWIM *stop* Fiona Lamb.'

NC had to be Nate Clatworthy. The details, I guessed, would be his address, date of birth, and maybe – just *maybe* – anything else the officials might need to know, like, for instance, who would be accompanying him on the pilot boat.

Before I could read the telegram again, Lena snatched it back, hastily refolding it.

'Someone's coming!' she hissed. 'Act normal.'

The door opened. There, in the hallway, was the last person I expected to see.

'I... I was just leaving,' Ma Blackwell stuttered, clearly taken aback. 'What are the horses doing here? More to the point, what are *you* doing here?'

I was wondering the same thing about her.

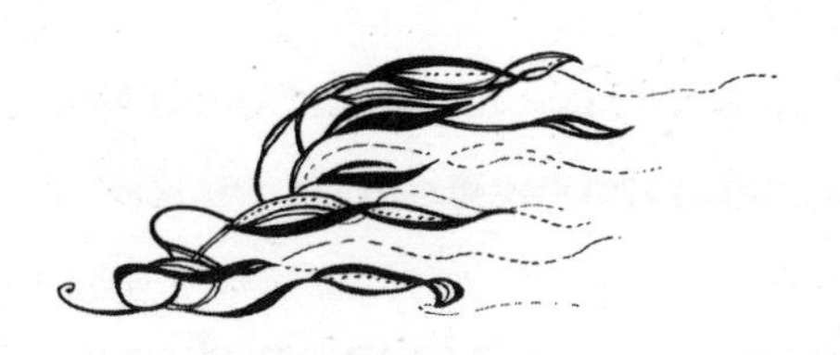

14.
SPRING, 1952
NELLIE

It was obvious we'd interrupted something. Ma Blackwell was uncharacteristically nervous, her eyes darting over us and back into the house again. Equally uncharacteristically, Lena was suddenly unsure what to say.

'Telegram for the captain,' I announced. 'Mrs Lee asked us to deliver it.'

Ma Blackwell wiped her hands on her pinny. As she reached for the telegram, Lena took a step back.

'Weren't you just leaving, Mrs Blackwell?' she said, finding her voice again and smiling sweetly. 'Because we wouldn't want to hold you up.'

'I am, thank you, pert miss,' Ma Blackwell snapped, trying once more to take the message.

Lena passed it to me, and I held it behind my back. Fate had handed us a brilliant opportunity, and I wasn't about to surrender it. All we had to do was persuade the captain to let me go on the pilot boat and write it in his reply.

'We're to deliver it in person. Captain Farley has to reply straight away,' I explained, being a little generous with the truth.

Ma Blackwell folded her arms, brow darkening. She was beginning to look more like her usual self, which was actually quite a relief.

'Why's it fallen to you two? Where's the delivery boy?' she demanded.

I explained about the chickenpox and tried to keep calm, though my heart was thundering away.

'So if you'll let us in . . .' I said, mounting the step.

'Very well.' Though Ma Blackwell didn't move straight away. 'He's in the library, so in and out quickly, and no nosing at anything that doesn't concern you.'

'We won't,' I assured her.

She stepped aside and we rushed in before she could change her mind.

The downstairs passage was full of boxes and tea chests. Upstairs, in the main entrance hall, it hit me properly: the house, as I remembered it, was almost unrecognisable. Everything was packed away or shrouded in dust sheets. There were patches on the walls where the pictures had been, water stains around the leaking windows, cobwebs on the beautiful vaulted ceiling. The smell was different too, not of furniture polish and dogs, as it had on my visits here with Mam, but of old, musty damp.

'Blimey, it's like an ancient castle!' Lena whispered.

'Smells like one too.' I wondered if anyone had cleaned since Mam died, because it certainly didn't look like it.

At the library door, I hesitated.

'I'm just going to ask him outright,' I whispered. 'I want to go on the pilot boat because—'

'Nate's specially requested you – his training buddy – to be there to support him,' Lena finished for me.

'I'm his lucky mascot.'

Lena gave me a nudge. 'Hey, *I'm* the lucky mascot round here.'

It suddenly struck me: if I was the one doing the swim, *I* needed *her* on the pilot boat to support me.

'Will you come too? Oh, say you will!' I pressed.

'Let's see if he agrees to you going first,' Lena replied. Yet I knew from the gleam in her eye that she'd jump at the chance.

Entering the library, my heart sped up all over again. It wasn't just nerves: it was being in this room, its huge windows so dull with dirt that what daylight was coming in made it already seem underwater. Last time I'd been in here was just a week before Mam died. It was a cold January day, I remembered, and as Mam was dusting the books I'd been charged with filling the coal scuttle and building up the fires. Soon these bookshelves, these fireplaces, would be lost for ever at the bottom of a lake.

Captain Farley was in the far corner, taking books from their shelves and packing them into boxes. He too was surprised to see us, though quickly recovered when we gave him the telegram.

'Only one slot left to swim in June, eh?' he said, on reading it.

Now was the moment to ask about the pilot boat, except I couldn't quite get the words out and dithered awkwardly.

The captain frowned at me. 'Is there something else you wanted?'

'Ummm . . . sir . . .' I swallowed. 'Is there a chance I could go on the—'

'Pilot boat, as Nate's support?' Captain Farley interrupted. 'Why, that makes perfect sense. I was going to suggest it, as it happens.'

'What? Oh!' I'd not expected this at all. It took a moment to sink in. 'Gosh, I mean, thank you, sir!'

'Told you it was a good plan,' Lena whispered. She was grinning her head off. All we needed now was for the Channel Swimming people to agree to the request, and the swap really would stand a chance of happening.

'Yes, well.' The captain looked slightly embarrassed. 'Is that all? Only I've plenty to be getting on with here.'

Putting the telegram down, he scooped up a pile of books.

'*Telegram!*' Lena hissed, nudging me.

I stepped forward. 'We'll deliver your reply to the post office, sir, so it goes off today, if you like?'

He glanced helplessly at the books piled up in his arms.

I seized the moment.

'We can write it for you too,' I offered.

I caught Lena's eye. This was our chance to add her name to the request: asking outright might've been pushing our luck.

'Ah, yes, good thinking. It does seem as if they'd like our reply urgently. You'll find a pen somewhere.' He waved vaguely in the direction of his desk, before returning to his bookshelves.

I rushed to the desk, finding a pen underneath some official-looking papers. I didn't mean to read them, but Ma Blackwell's name was on the top sheet of paper. And so was mine. And a signature, the ink still glossy, as if not quite dry. It looked like a receipt for a payment – swimming club fees, probably. Which I supposed explained why Ma Blackwell had been here, getting a refund now I no longer swam at the lido every week.

'Hurry up!' Lena whispered.

I moved away from the desk.

'Thank you, again, sir!' I called over my shoulder.

We both practically ran for the door.

*

At a safe distance from the house, and on a grassy bank where the horses could graze, we stopped to compose our reply. Lena, who had clearer handwriting than me, said she'd write everything so long as I told her what to say. My face ached from smiling so hard.

'I can't believe it!' I gushed.

'Well, it's truly happening,' Lena replied, the captain's pen poised, tip of her tongue pressed against her teeth in concentration. 'Okay, what shall I put?'

I took a steadying breath.

'Right, how about: "Nate . . . no . . . NC requests training partners Nellie Foster and Lena Gill on pilot boat. *stop*—"'

Lena smiled. 'Yup. What else?'

'No parents on board, no Mrs Lamb. "NC requests Captain Farley as only adult. *stop*." The fewer people who'll recognise us when we swap, the better,' I explained.

'How should we end it?'

'"Please confirm the above and inform us of exact swim date and time ASAP. *stop*."'

Lena wrote everything down, telegram pressed against her leg, then read it through again.

'Hmm . . .' She looked thoughtful. 'Are you sure you want the captain there?'

'They'll expect us to have a grown-up, won't they? He's the best of the bunch.'

'True. You know, I bet he still thinks it should be you doing the swim.'

I shrugged: all that business of who was the best swimmer or who should've been picked mattered less now we'd taken matters into our own hands.

Lena checked the message before handing it to me. I checked it too, hardly believing what we were doing.

It was probably wrong to forge a telegram. Probably wrong to lie to Mrs Lamb and the Channel Swimming people. And even now, being included on the crew of the pilot boat was only the first step of our daring, difficult plan. Yet everything else about this felt utterly right. When I swam I became a different person. I was no longer an orphan without a true family or home. I wasn't ordinary. I had a talent – a real, special talent of the kind most people could only dream of.

What *was* wrong was not using that talent to help Nate escape the school bullies. And if the swim was done in June, the money I might earn from it would set Lena and me up for good. No one would say they couldn't afford us then.

I slipped the telegram in my pocket, picked up the reins and urged Perry on. Lena rode alongside me. Now, at last, we tucked into the sugar mice.

'You'd better still be my friend when you're world famous,' Lena said, biting the nose off a pink mouse.

I laughed, eating the rump of my white one. 'Course I will, don't be daft.'

'It's true, though, everyone'll know who you are: Nellie Foster, first kid swimmer of the Channel. It'll be your picture on people's walls, not Gertrude Ederle's.'

To be honest, this part worried me almost as much as the plan itself. I couldn't imagine what it would be like to see my face all over the papers.

'You'll just have to plait my hair super-duper nicely, won't you?' I said to Lena.

'Only if I can have another pink sugar mouse,' she replied.

There was only one left in the bag, but I wasn't about to argue.

15.
LATE SPRING, 1952
NELLIE

I'd hoped we'd get a quick reply to the telegram. We needed to know the exact date for the swim, and the closer to the sixteenth of June deadline it was, the better. Yet a week passed with no news. Then another. The waiting dragged on – and on – and became almost painful.

'Have you heard from the Channel Swimming people?' I asked the captain, who, despite moving away from Syndercombe, was now turning up at training at least once a week.

'It'll take a while to arrange everything,' he replied.

'But it's already *been* three weeks,' I argued.

'Patience, Nellie,' he warned. 'Your job is to help Nate get into good shape so we're ready when they give the word. Concentrate on that, please.'

So I tried my best to put it from my mind.

Meanwhile, though Ma Blackwell never said why she'd been at the captain's house that day, very soon afterwards she took me aside to tell me everything was sorted. When she and Mr Blackwell left Syndercombe I could indeed carry on living with them, for good.

My first reaction was of huge relief.

'And Lena?' I asked hopefully. 'Can she come too?' A simple yes from Ma Blackwell would take the pressure off needing the sponsorship money. I'd still do the swim, still help Nate, but it'd be a huge thing to not have to worry about.

Her answer, though, was unchanged.

'Now, Nellie. We've already discussed this. Lena should be with her own family.'

'But Lena's almost *our* family nowadays,' I pleaded. 'Don't make her go. We'll do the horses every night – and every morning – and we'll do all the dishes, and dig the potatoes, and—'

'There won't be any horses when we move,' Ma Blackwell interrupted. 'Perry and Sage are being sold.'

I didn't believe her. Mr Blackwell wouldn't let that happen.

'Everyone's got tractors these days,' she tried to

explain. 'And we won't be farming any more, not like we do here.'

'But he loves his horses!' I cried. *I* loved his horses.

'And he knows when it's right to let them go.' Ma Blackwell's face was closed. 'I'm sorry, Nellie, but that's how it is.'

'You know Lena still coughs in the night, sometimes?' I said, trying a different tack.

'Listen to me, will you?' Ma Blackwell was losing patience. 'We can't afford to raise two children. It costs money.'

So why didn't the rest of the world share this view? I wondered. People were having babies all the time. We kept seeing pregnant women on the bus, in the village, in town. The newspapers had even given it a name – the baby boom – and like everything else seemed to be, said it was all down to the war.

'Lena *has* to go home by the June deadline.' Ma Blackwell was firm.

I went straight upstairs to our bedroom, and to Lena, who was lying on her counterpane, reading a letter from her mother.

'The Blackwells are selling Perry and Sage,' I told her, by now on the verge of tears.

Lena was horrified. 'Not the horses!'

I nodded miserably.

'Oh, Nellie.'

She beckoned me to come and sit beside her. She knew how much I loved Perry, and it was some comfort to be with the one person who understood. Mr Blackwell might be willing to give up his horses, but I'd never leave Lena. Doing the swim, earning the sponsorship deal, was our only way to ensure we'd be together.

But all this not knowing about the date was properly frustrating. What made it worse was watching the village pack up around us as the June deadline inched ever closer. Over half of Syndercombe's houses now stood empty. Soon they'd be starting work on clearing the graveyard and taking the bodies to the new cemetery in town, and that meant moving Mam. It was another thing I was dreading.

*

Despite the stress of waiting for news, the training was going well. So too was the momentum behind the swim, which was building every day in new and exciting ways. One Saturday morning a photographer came to take publicity shots of Nate and he made us promise to be there.

'We're going to support him,' I reminded Lena – and myself – as we dressed in our smartest frocks and tidied our hair.

'And to have a nose at where he lives,' Lena replied.

The meeting was at the Clatworthys' huge house in the next valley, the front door of which was answered by a woman wearing an apron.

'Crikey, has he got a *maid*?' I hissed. Lena tried not to giggle.

We were shown into a sitting room full of flowery chairs and sofas, and actual flowers tastefully arranged in vases. The Clatworthys were in a group by the fireplace, talking to a lady wearing a camera around her neck.

'Hi, come on in! I'm Sophie, by the way.' She beamed.

Captain Farley was there too, I noticed, browsing someone else's bookshelves this time. Lena and I perched on a sofa to watch as Sophie clicked away with her camera.

'We're awfully proud of him,' said Mrs Clatworthy, pretty in a grey silk dress. 'Such an achievement for a child his age.'

'Indeed, he has a remarkable talent for swimming,' Mr Clatworthy agreed smugly.

I felt myself reddening at this. Captain Farley coughed, and I'd a sudden, terrible fear that he'd somehow guessed the truth of the situation. As more praise was heaped on Nate, I grew hotter, and probably redder, until thankfully, his little brother Eddie decided to pick his nose. Horrified, Mrs Clatworthy rushed to fetch a hanky. The photo session came to an end.

'Thanks for coming,' said Nate, flopping on to the sofa beside us. 'Phew! I'm glad that's done.'

'I don't believe it is, quite,' Captain Farley remarked, then to Sophie: 'Did you not require a shot of the support crew?'

She agreed she did.

And so we went outside to stand around the Clatworthys' garden pond. Though I tried to hide behind Lena, Captain Farley insisted I be at the front with Nate. Lena stood very slightly behind us. Nate was a natural before the camera, that star quality Mrs Lamb had recognised shining out of him. In contrast, I felt awkward and embarrassed. It was the first time I'd had my photo taken properly, though if our plan for the swim worked, it wouldn't be the last. I knew I'd have to get used to cameras and photographers.

'I suppose even Gertrude Ederle had to start somewhere,' I admitted on the walk home.

'Still, it was nice of Captain Farley to make sure you had your photo taken, wasn't it?' Lena remarked.

I hadn't thought of it like that.

*

The following week, Captain Farley moved our Saturday training session to the seaside. By now it was May, and there'd still been no word of an exact date for the swim. If it wasn't decided soon, before the deadline to leave Syndercombe, Lena would have to go back to London. Time was running out.

The Bristol Channel coast was seven miles from the village. It wasn't the nicest stretch of coastline, with grey shale beaches, mud flats and water the colour of rain clouds, but it presented us with challenges we'd not yet faced. Another would be swimming under the watchful eyes of Captain Farley, Mrs Lamb, who'd flown in from America, *and* our sponsor, the chewing gum man, Mr Wrigley, who was keen to check Nate's progress.

At six o'clock on a damp morning, we gathered on the beach. The sea was choppy, the breeze a brisk north-westerly. Nate and I were nervous. Although I wore my costume under my clothes just in case, it was Nate they'd come to see, Nate who shivered in his black tunic and orange cap, and whose training had mostly been, these past weeks, the short bike ride to and from the gravel pits. Lena, provider of encouraging thumbs ups and cheering smiles, watched from the sidelines.

Mrs Lamb wasted no time in explaining to Mr Wrigley why Nate was such an extraordinary find.

'He's charming, likeable, photographs like a natural. You've seen the shots Sophie took,' she said.

'Sure,' Mr Wrigley agreed. 'We've got ourselves a proper young English gentleman, eh? People are going to love him!'

Though he looked unremarkable in a grey suit and glasses, Mr Wrigley's American accent made it hard not to be excited by the glamour of it all. He and Mrs Lamb talked about photographs, television, magazine articles as if they were auditioning a movie star.

Eventually, almost as an afterthought, the conversation turned to the swim.

'You've had the June date confirmed?' Mrs Lamb asked Captain Farley. 'The association's been in touch?'

I shot him a nervous glance in case he'd heard and not told us.

The captain shook his head.

'Really?' Mrs Lamb was surprised and slightly annoyed. 'Too many requests, that's the problem. I've never known Channel swimming be so popular. Leave it with me. I'll chase it up.'

Her attention then turned to Nate. 'You've built up your stamina? You've been training?'

He assured her he'd worked very hard indeed.

'You've been eating well, I see. Lots of carbohydrates,' she remarked.

'Yup.' Nate gave his stomach a prod. 'That wasn't too hard.'

I smiled.

'But the training on your own? How's that going?'

Nate caught my eye. 'Actually, I didn't.'

'Aha!' Mrs Lamb glanced from Nate to me in understanding. '*You're* the secret weapon, are you?'

I nodded, suddenly shy.

'Nellie's a top-notch training partner,' Captain Farley put in. 'They train together most of the time, and we've requested that she be on the pilot boat. What do you say they swim together today, as it's their first sea session?'

Mrs Lamb's mouth twitched: as she considered the request, I held my breath.

'Very well,' she said.

Mr Wrigley shrugged. 'Sure, sounds peachy to me.'

I breathed again, and in a flash I was down to my costume, tugging on my orange cap.

'You'll have to gauge the waves,' Mrs Lamb told us. 'And keep your mouth closed. Too much saline will make you as sick as a dog. Your skin will be sore afterwards too. Being in salt water for a long time does strange things to the body.'

I listened carefully. Nate, though, was impatient to get in the water.

'Race you in,' Nate whispered to me.

'NO RACING!' Captain Farley barked. 'Conserve your energy!'

It surprised me just how different it was to swim in the sea after the gravel pits. The water was heavier, more unpredictable, and tasted absolutely vile. There were times when I surged ahead of Nate, and times when I held back so as not to raise too much suspicion. After two hours, we were called in.

'Well done,' I said, passing Nate his towel.

But the swim had taken it out of him: his eyes were bloodshot. He was shuddering with cold. I could've easily kept swimming, and as we walked back up the beach, Captain Farley fell in beside me.

'Good swim, Nellie,' he said quietly. 'You'll do well.'

I wasn't sure what he meant. Was he talking about a time in the future when I might make my own attempt to the swim the Channel? Or had he twigged what we were planning for June?

I didn't dare to ask.

*

True to her word, Mrs Lamb did chase things up. Only a few days later at the end of school, we saw Nate waiting for us at the school gates.

'Nellie! Lena! Guess what I've got!' he hollered, waving an envelope above his head

I clutched Lena's hand. 'Oh, thank heck! They've replied!'

'To Nate? Not the captain?' Lena asked.

'They probably wrote to him too. Anyway, Nate's the one doing the swim—'

'Or so they think . . .' Lena replied, eyes glinting with delight.

We elbowed through the usual crowd of kids all dying to be the first out of the gates, to where Nate was waiting on the pavement. He was splattered with mud – and cow dung, from the smell of him – and had clearly run all the way across the fields from his house.

'Here, you read it,' he insisted, handing the envelope to me.

The letter was still sealed, and from the outside looked as plain as the coal merchant's bill. That didn't stop my stomach from giving a queasy, fluttery turn. *Please be good news*, I begged silently, before ripping the envelope open.

The letter was on smart, headed paper from the Swimming Association. It was addressed to N. Clatworthy, and stated Nate's registration number, the start date – Monday 23rd June – the time of the swim – 2.00 a.m. – and the place where, weather permitting, he'd enter the water at Dover.

'"You must wait for a sign from your pilot before walking into the sea",' I read out to the others. '"Your entry point will be Shakespeare Beach, your destination Cap Gris-Nez, France. On arrival at the French coast you will be expected to leave the water on foot and take three steps on dry land for the swim to be valid."'

'What about you, Nellie? What does it say about you coming?' Nate asked anxiously.

'I'm getting to that bit.' I ran my finger down the page. '"The pilot will be Johnny Hawkins on his boat, the *Maybelle*. Places on board are also confirmed for principal trainer Captain Farley and training partners Nellie Foster—"'

'*Yes!*' Nate punched the air.

'"And",' I continued, my hands now shaking, '"Lena Gill."'

Lena swayed slightly. 'Holy mackerel!' she whispered. 'It's really happening!'

I looked at Nate, at Lena.

'I think we did it, didn't we?!' I said.

Nate beamed. 'By jove, old thing, I think we did!'

16.
LATE SPRING, 1952
NELLIE

The news gave us a whopping great boost. With only a week between the village deadline and the swim, I felt pretty confident Ma Blackwell would give in and let Lena stay on with us a bit longer. Yet she still took some persuading.

'We'll have moved by then, mind, so there might not be much room.'

'It's only for a few nights. We can sleep top to toe in the same bed,' I pleaded.

'So you're *both* going on the boat to support Nate, eh? Well, in't he the lucky chap.' Ma Blackwell's brows bristled with suspicion. She still wasn't a fan of Nate's.

I grew frustrated. 'Well? *Can* Lena stay? Please say she can.'

'If her father says so, I suppose,' Ma Blackwell finally

agreed. 'He'll need to know she's off to France in a boat, remember. There might be paperwork to do.'

*

Once Lena had penned a quick letter to her dad, we didn't think much more about it, not when there was so much else happening. It was, by now, the end of May, and as we trained harder than ever, life in Syndercombe was nearing its end.

First, that same week, our village school closed. There were only twenty pupils, though in the war there'd been evacuees, and before that generations of local families like the Blackwells and the Sethertons, going right back to Victorian times. We were taught in the one classroom, which served as an assembly space, a dinner hall and the library. After next week, all that would change. We'd be going to West Birchwood, a small town in the next valley, which had a junior and secondary school, and was where the older kids like Maudie went already.

Though I was excited about the new school, leaving Miss Setherton and Syndercombe was a real wrench. Lena was sympathetic, but also rather astonished.

'Honestly, Nell, I've never seen anyone cry so much over leaving school,' she admitted.

I'd only just recovered by Thursday, when the undertakers arrived to clear the churchyard. Since that night back in February, of the first meeting at the village hall, I'd been dreading this moment. A smattering of villagers had gathered to watch proceedings, among them Captain Farley, whose car was parked on the roadside. A canvas screen had been erected near the lychgate, so we couldn't see what was happening. But we heard the slap and slice of spades digging soil, and wheelbarrows full of the stuff kept appearing from behind the screen.

They'd already cleared some of the headstones. The ones still intact were propped up against the church wall, but plenty more had been split, chipped – half a word here, a cherub's wing there – lying like builders' rubble on the pavement. I couldn't bear for Mam's headstone to be treated this way. We'd had to empty her post office savings account to pay for it, a rectangle of polished granite and the words 'Mary Foster: dearest mam to Nellie'. If it got broken, I'd never afford a new one, and so decided it was best to act now.

'I'm going to fetch Mam's gravestone,' I told Lena.

'You're *what*?' She pulled a puzzled face. 'How're you going to get it home?'

'You're going to help me.'

Behind the screen the churchyard was a mess of open trenches and mud. It was bad enough that the dead were being sent to a cemetery miles from where they'd lived. But this carelessness, this lack of respect made me angry. Mam's plot was easy to spot, being one of the only headstones in her row still upright. The relief was short-lived, though. What was left of her grave was a deep, empty pit: the coffin had already been taken. The shock of it made me start crying.

'Nellie,' Lena warned, as one of the workmen approached. I quickly wiped my eyes.

'You're not supposed to be here,' the workman informed us. 'Scarper or I'll call the site manager.'

I lifted my chin in what I hoped was a brave manner. 'This is my mam's gravestone, and I'll be taking it to the cemetery myself, please,' I explained.

'You can't do that,' the man replied.

'It's my property: my family paid for it, so it's mine,' I insisted.

'Not any more. The water board owns everything in this valley, right down to your front door handle.'

I didn't believe him. Surely, the brassware on Combe Grange's door belonged to the Blackwells. And Mam's gravestone was definitely mine. I tried to argue with the man, but he wasn't budging and I was too upset to stand my ground. Reluctantly, I followed Lena back out to the street.

'You don't suppose he'd help?' Lena asked, meaning Captain Farley, who also appeared to be upset over the broken headstones.

The group of workmen he was addressing stared shamefully at their boots.

'You're meant to move the headstones, not obliterate them!' the captain boomed. 'What the hell's got into you? Have you lost all respect?'

'We're only following orders,' one of the workmen tried to say.

'Which is what the Nazis said,' the captain retorted. 'I've a good mind to report the lot of you to Mr Clatworthy, and insist he takes the cost of this from your wages.'

All the time he'd been speaking, Lena had drifted towards him. Finally, he looked up and saw us – saw me, my face streaked with tears.

'Oh, Nellie, this is most unfortunate. Has your mother's gravestone suffered the same fate?' he asked.

'Not yet,' I croaked. 'But they won't let me take it away. They say it belongs to the water board.'

'Do they indeed?' He straightened his spine. 'We'll see about that.'

Captain Farley disappeared behind the canvas screen. In next to no time, he reappeared with Mam's headstone in a wheelbarrow.

I was stunned.

'Do return the wheelbarrow when you're done, won't you?' he said briskly.

'Of course.' I seized the handles. 'Thank you, sir!'

The captain waved away my gratitude. 'Think nothing of it.'

But of course, we did, and discussed it all the way back to Combe Grange.

'I can't believe the captain did that for me,' I said, pushing the wheelbarrow over the cobbles.

'I can,' Lena replied.

'Can you? Why?'

'He's always nice to you, Nell. Makes a bit of a fuss of you.'

'Does he?'

I could feel a flush creeping up my neck. The captain *was* often kind to me. I was aware of it too: he'd let me come to the hall with Mam all those times, and took a special interest in my swimming. If any grown-up had to be involved in our training then I was glad it was him.

Lena gave me a playful jab with her elbow. '*Papa* material, maybe?'

'*What?*' I stopped, bewildered.

We'd not played our game for ages and it took me a moment to realise what she was up to. Thankfully, Miss Setherton was on the opposite side of the street, so I was able to get in a quick '*Mama*' in retaliation.

'Seriously, though, Nell. Don't you ever wonder who your dad is, or was?' Lena asked.

'But I know what happened,' I reminded her: I'd told her all this before, in one of our late-night chats. 'He was a soldier who didn't come home from the war.'

I set off again, pushing the wheelbarrow in a very determined fashion. What did Lena mean, bringing up my father like that?

'Sorry, I didn't mean to upset you,' Lena said, struggling to keep pace with me.

I sighed. 'It's just that I don't know much else about him. I never knew him. It's different with Mam: there's tons I remember.'

'Okay, tell me something about her, then.'

I liked this idea better. 'Well, she loved gooseberry jam, and could crack open walnuts with her teeth.'

'Wow!'

'What about yours?' I asked.

Lena smiled warmly. 'She'd sing to me. Change the words to silly ones. She called me Le-Le.'

'*Calls*,' I corrected her. 'She's not dead.'

'No, she's not. And even if she was she'd still be alive in me, wouldn't she?'

I'd not thought of it like that before, but Lena was right. Though our mothers weren't actually here, they were with us in our faces, our smiles, the way our hair fell, our laughter, our courage to not give up. And after the shock of seeing Mam's empty grave, this was a comfort.

'Thanks, Lena,' I said. 'For understanding. For being such a terrific pal.'

She laid her head on my shoulder. 'Likewise.'

We walked on in silence, only slowing as we approached Combe Grange. The Blackwells had, by now, found a new place to move into, a cottage up at Marley's Head that was smaller, with proper heating and lino on the floors. There was hardly any garden to speak of. Mr Blackwell's apple tree saplings that he'd salvaged from the orchard would have to be replanted in a friend's field further down the lane.

'We all have to make do,' Ma Blackwell pointed out. Yet I couldn't imagine ever loving it like I did Combe Grange.

'I'm going to miss living here,' Lena said, staring up at the old farmhouse.

'Gosh, me too.'

In the giddy whirl of the last hour or so, I'd almost forgotten the goodbyes we still had to say, to the horses, to the village, to the church. I felt as if my heart would burst.

And here was Combe Grange, as close to home as anywhere had been for me. It was looking particularly lovely in the early summer sunshine, the stone mellow pink, the thatch alive with sparrows and martins, and the thick glass of the windows warping the light like oil. Earlier that day, Lena had swept the steps and polished our usually mud-splattered front door. Now it looked spotless, the brassware on the door – the handle, the letter box, the knocker – all shining to perfection.

'You'd be lucky to live in such a fine house, wouldn't you?' Lena observed, taking my hand.

I nodded. We were.

17.
SUMMER, 2032
POLLY

Joel's still here as I stumble out of the lake. He's sitting on the ground, looking lost.

'Gave up on the swimming idea, huh?' he asks.

I don't answer because I'm concentrating on getting the water out of my ears: it buys me a moment to take in what's just happened. I glance at my wet clothes and think I should be wearing a cap and costume because Nellie wouldn't be impressed. I still feel Lena's hand holding mine, and can hear Nate calling out 'old thing!' in his funny posh voice. So the fact it's Joel talking to me, and I'm Polly again, takes a minute to get used to. The door handle is in my pocket: from the feel of it, it's closed. The time travel, I'm understanding now, happens at two in the morning because that's when the village had to be emptied, and when Nate's Channel swim was due to start.

An ending and a beginning.

'You had something to tell me, Joel,' I remember. 'About why you've been miserable.'

'So I did.'

'It's not about Mum, is it? Her being ill?'

'What?' He looks momentarily puzzled. 'No, not that.'

I'm relieved.

'That night we went to the beach, Pol,' he begins.

My stomach drops. *This* again.

'I wasn't just going swimming,' he says. 'Afterwards, I was planning on getting the early morning train to London.'

'*London?*' But he doesn't know anyone in London. 'What for?'

'To get away from Brighton. To go to college.'

I'm confused. 'Hang on. You were leaving us? Leaving home?'

He half shrugs, half nods. 'There's a college in London I want to try out.'

I feel slightly dizzy. I've never heard about any *college*. Never heard Mum and Dad speaking about it. Anyway, Joel's only fifteen. And who leaves for a college course in the middle of the night?

'I don't get it,' I say.

Joel leans back on his hands. 'I don't want to go to school any more, Pol.'

'Well, you *definitely* can't leave home!' I say, on the brink of tears.

'I'm still here, aren't I?'

But in my mind's eye I see him climbing over our balcony. As well as the towel, he was carrying a bag – an overnight bag. The same one he said was already packed when we were getting ready to come here. I'm in pieces.

'You're not going to try it again, are you? Tell me you're not!' I beg. Though why *wouldn't* he run away when everything's been awful since the clip got posted.

There's a horribly long pause.

'I haven't decided yet,' Joel admits.

'Arrrgghhh!' I scream. This is all so rubbish and stupid and *wrong*. At least in Syndercombe, Nate ran away *back to* his family. 'You can't just leave Mum and Dad, or me!'

'You're forgetting someone. The person who has to put up with the snide comments, being made to feel like nothing.' He points to himself. 'Me.'

I actually can't think what to say.

Joel gets to his feet. 'Come on. It's easier to talk when you're walking.'

We make our way across the lake bed, back towards

Jessie's, and sure enough, it seems to loosen Joel's tongue.

'If you had a special talent,' he begins, 'and it was important to you – I'm talking *serious*, fire-in-the-belly, can't-live-without-it important – what would you do?'

'As you know, I'm pretty average at most things,' I admit, though I'm not sure how underwater time travelling fits into this. With Nellie, her talent's obviously swimming. But Nate's good at all sorts: cooking eggs, swimming, knowing the right thing to say to our new downstairs neighbour, getting decent grades.

'Go on, then,' I say. 'What's your "fire-in-the-belly" talent?'

'Dance.'

I glance at him in case he's joking. But his face is serious, unsmiling.

'What, like tap, ballet, ballroom—' I can't think of any more types, though I do remember going to dance classes with Joel when we were little, and him being so much better at it than me. I'd no idea he still did dance: I suppose it must be at school.

'All of it,' he says.

'Really?'

'Yes, *really*.'

'Oh . . . I mean . . . wow, that's pretty amazing.'

'Go on, say it – it's not exactly a useful talent.'

'Don't put words into my mouth! I just didn't know you were into dance, that's all.'

He stuffs his hands into his pockets. 'Well, I am, all right?'

It occurs to me that this is what he's been up to in his room all summer, headphones on, counting beats, jumping about until Miss Gee complains and tells us we have feet like Clydesdale horses – like Perry and Sage, I think.

'So this college in London—' I begin.

'Is a specialist dance school,' he finishes. 'And it costs money.'

'Which Mum and Dad don't have,' I say, following. 'But Joel – you haven't got money, either.'

'No, but there's this scholarship I can get next year—'

'Next *year*?'

'So this year I'd have to get a job or something.'

I pull a baffled face.

'I *know* it's a stupid idea! Thanks for pointing that out!' Joel cries in frustration. 'But I'm not going back to that school, Pol. No. Way.'

He means it.

So did Nate, who was so desperate he took on a swimming challenge that was way beyond him. Luckily he had Nellie and Lena wanting to help. There must be some way I can make things better for Joel.

'What can I do?' I ask. 'Anything. Tell me.'

Joel gives a miserable half shrug. 'Just keep it to yourself, all right? I'm trusting you with this one.'

We walk on, the quiet tense between us. I feel sick and panicky. Really, I should warn Mum and Dad that he's refusing to go back to school next week, but if I do I'm letting Joel down.

It's then I remember: Joel knew who was on the pier that night, didn't he? Or at least, he had an idea. This wasn't really about my terrible swimming; it never was. It's about my brother being good at something, and someone else not liking it. That someone, I wouldn't mind betting, is the same person whose name he couldn't give the teachers, who's been bullying him all this time at school.

*

When I open my eyes the next morning, the light is different. For the first time in ages the sun isn't shining. It's already too hot to breathe. In the kitchen, I'm relieved to see Joel at the breakfast table. *He's still here,* I think. Except it's not that straightforward, is it? My brother's got big dreams, and if there's one thing Nellie's taught me it's that he's right to want to go after them. Even if it *is* complicated.

'The forecast says it's going to thunder,' says Jessie.

'And rain?' I ask.

'Fingers crossed.'

'Petrichor,' Joel mumbles into his cereal, before lifting his bowl to drink the sludge at the bottom. 'It's that smell you get when it's been dry for ages and then it rains.'

'Is that right, Einstein?' Jessie gets up and ruffles his hair, which he normally hates.

This morning he doesn't duck away from her hand, which makes me hope he's feeling better now he's told me what's been happening, and think that maybe I should, in the spirit of trading secrets, tell him about Syndercombe. Perhaps it might help him to hear about Nate, and know that you don't have to put up with bullies, that the best people are the ones on your side. The jazzy ringtone on Jessie's device interrupts my thinking.

'Hi, Liz,' she says. It's a video call from Mum. 'Wait a sec . . . you're in *hospital*?'

I leap up, rush to Jessie's side. Joel does the same, and the three of us crowd around the screen. Last time we saw Mum she was heading back to bed: it's a bit of a jump to now be seeing her in a hospital gown with a drip in the back of her hand.

'What's happened?' I cry.

'Is it heatstroke?' Joel asks.

'Are you really, seriously ill?' I'm suddenly thinking of Nellie's mother. 'Because if you're going to die then could you please at least warn us so we can try to be ready.'

'Pol, love, I got dehydrated, that's all. I was never this sick with you two, and I wasn't going to tell you yet, until we were sure everything was okay. But . . .' Mum falters. '. . . I'm pregnant.'

Jessie stiffens. 'Oh, Liz, you're not!'

It's only now I begin to take this in. Mum doesn't look especially ill. In fact she's smiling, in a slightly embarrassed way. Dad's there with her, and has the same expression on his face.

'I know what I said about having babies, Jessie,' Mum admits. 'We didn't plan for it to happen.'

She lays her hand – the one that's all taped up with the needle in it – on her tummy. Despite the rest of her being very slim, her tummy is round and tight . . . and totally, utterly, surprisingly HUGE. I can't believe I'd not noticed it before. I'm in shock. I'm laughing too because this is amazing. I've always wanted a little brother or sister, but it never occurred to me our family might get bigger.

I stare at Mum's belly. 'So there's really a baby in there?'

Joel rolls his eyes at me. My parents laugh. It's only Jessie who doesn't seem delighted at the news.

'Here.' She hands me the device. 'I've got to get ready for work, sorry.'

Once she's out of the room, Mum holds a blurry, black-and-white scan picture up to the screen. I'm trying to focus and hold the device steady. It's a heck of a lot to get my head round.

'She's got your dad's knobbly knees,' Mum says.

'*She?*' Joel groans. 'Not another sister?'

Joel and I pore over the photo. We can clearly see her skull, her nose and lips, her legs bunched against her chest. Mixed in with the surprise of all this, I'm over the moon.

'Hope she hasn't got your curly mop, poor kid,' Joel says, laughing.

For once I don't mind the mention of my hair. All I think is: *I've got a sister! Wow!*

'Yeah, well, yours is the same, curly-wurly,' I remind him.

The call ends soon after that, and Joel and I sit down, stunned. Jessie reappears, hair pinned up ready for work, her nurse ID swinging from her neck. She looks upset, I think, red cheeked and angry, and thumps about the kitchen, filling her water bottle and choosing fruit from the bowl.

'It's irresponsible, that's what it is,' she says, obviously meaning the new baby. 'Liz has already got you two, which should be enough, shouldn't it?'

Joel shrugs, embarrassed. He takes his bowl to the sink, washes it and goes outside. I'm left facing my aunt alone, already knowing what she thinks about people bringing babies into our overheating, overcrowded world.

'I *am* quite excited about having a little sister,' I admit. 'I know it's another mouth to feed and—'

'*Another mouth?*' Jessie turns to me. 'You do realise that by the time your little sister is your age these heatwaves will be happening every single summer, and it'll probably be too hot for people to keep living on the south coast of England?'

I gulp. No, I didn't realise, not this soon.

'It's going to happen, Pol, all across the world – places becoming too hot to live in, and millions of people on the move, trying to find somewhere cooler, trying to survive.'

'You're making it sound like what happened to Syndercombe!' I cry.

Jessie throws up her arms. 'It *is* like Syndercombe! That's exactly what happens when our world gets too greedy and people want too much!'

'But didn't the towns need fresh water? Isn't that why the reservoir was built?' I argue, because most of the villagers seemed to accept this was the case, eventually.

'Towns that, after the war, were being filled with young families having babies, do you mean?' Jessie retorts, then sighs. 'I'm sorry, Pol, but babies aren't just cute and squishy. They don't make problems go away: they *can* cause them too.'

'So you're not happy for Mum?'

'I'm not happy *for the baby*,' she replies. 'Climate situation aside, your sister is going to be growing up in a tiny flat in Brighton with stressed-out parents who are trying to save their business. It's not exactly good timing, is it?'

Maybe not. But that's not my sister's fault, and I'm going to do all I can to make sure she feels welcomed into the world, and totally and utterly loved.

*

I go and find Joel in the garden. He, at least, seems happy at our baby sister news.

'It's a good reason to stick around,' I remind him. 'She'll need her big brother, Joel.'

Just like that his face closes, tight as a fist.

'Give it a rest, Pol, will you?' he says.

I go back inside. It's too hot to argue.

To turn down the noise in my head, I try doing my homework. It's hard to believe we'll be back at school in a few days, and since I have all my lessons with Sasha, I can't help wondering what that's going to be like if we're still not speaking. Not as bad as what Joel's going through, sure, but I'm not exactly looking forward to it.

I stare at the homework task:

Question 1: Looking back on your life, what have you achieved that you're proud of?

Question 2: Is there something in your life that you regret or that you'd change?

Mary, I think, would be perfect for this task. It's so frustrating not being able to ask her. In my head I put the questions to Nellie instead: *being a brilliant swimmer* she'd say for question one, I reckon, and *having to leave Syndercombe*, for question two. I still don't know if she ever did swim the Channel, or what happened after Syndercombe, or who was leaving the yellow roses.

Nor do I really know why all this is happening to me.

Sure, Nellie had great friends and an incredible talent

for swimming, and Nate – wealthy, privileged Nate – ran away from school because people there made fun of him for struggling with his literacy. If this whole strange experience is making me realise anything, it's that anyone's life, at any time, is going to have its tough times, even if it's not always obvious to everyone else.

I think about Sasha, who lives with her sister, mum and dad in a nice house, in a nice part of town. When's life ever been tough for her? Or maybe it has, and I've just not noticed. Perhaps that's what she meant when she said it wasn't all about me, and why she's disappeared online. I don't know.

Yet I *do* know, quite clearly, that if we, as people, don't look after each other and our animals and our countryside, then what else do we have? What else matters?

My mind flips back to my baby sister – already, I love her fiercely.

Two in the morning: a beginning and an ending.

Perhaps the baby is our family's new beginning. And if it is, then how does all this end? First, I need to know what happens to Nellie.

*

Just before two o'clock, when the house is asleep, I go down to the lake. It's darker tonight, the sky heavy, the moon hazy behind the clouds. Thankfully, at the water's edge there's no Joel this time, and I swim out to the deepest part, my stroke feeling surprisingly steady and strong. When my feet find the church roof, it almost feels warm, as if the sun has been shining on it. In my pocket, the door handle turns.

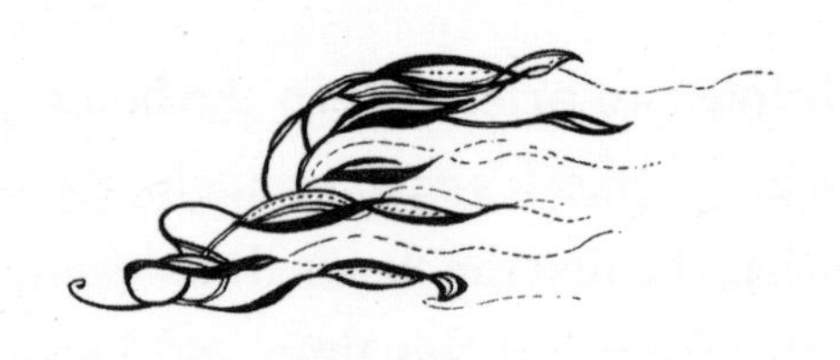

18.
EARLY SUMMER, 1952
NELLIE

I woke up, damp-cheeked and blinking. Our bedroom was full of summer sunshine, so bright I had to shield my eyes. Yesterday Ma Blackwell had taken down the curtains in order to pack them. Anything that wasn't for wearing or eating had been boxed up for the short journey to the new cottage at Marley's Head. Today, I remembered with a heart thud, was our last morning at Combe Grange. It hit me again how quickly everything was happening.

'What's the story, morning glory?' Lena mumbled from under her bedclothes.

It was a comfort to hear her voice.

'What's your tale, nightingale?' I answered.

Getting up, I stepped over Lena's suitcase lying open on the floor. Ma Blackwell had fetched it from the attic so she could start to pack her own things, and the sight of it gave me a sudden attack of nerves. Everything was in place for the swim swap to happen. Everything, so far, was going to plan, yet that didn't stop me worrying about how difficult it was going to be to pull off. And that was *before* I faced a gruelling twenty-mile swim that no child my age had ever managed.

A quick wash, a comb of my hair and I felt better. Or at least strong enough to face what I had to do next. Down in the kitchen, Ma Blackwell was making porridge. Since I'd started the new school at West Birchwood last week, she was more insistent than ever on the benefits of a solid breakfast. That morning, though, I hurried past her to go straight outside.

'Don't forget you've the school bus to catch,' she called after me.

Today was the day Perry and Sage were going to their new home, and it was time to say goodbye. The yard felt strangely empty. The late lambs and laying hens had gone to market, the early hay harvested, a dozen Cox's Pippin apple trees moved from the orchard and Mr Blackwell's farm equipment had been sold. All that was left were the horses.

A patter of feet behind me, and there was Lena, still tucking her blouse into her skirt.

'Don't say goodbye without me,' she pleaded, then, seeing how sad I was, linked arms. 'Come on, let's get them looking shipshape, shall we?'

The horses, expecting breakfast, appeared at their stable doors. Perry made his lovely whickering sound and Sage, ever impatient for her oats, stamped her hoof. Once they were fed, we brought them out into the yard, and groomed them until their summer coats gleamed like polished conkers. Lena also insisted on plaiting their manes and tails. By the time we'd finished they were as smart as show horses.

'You be good for your new owners, won't you?' I said to Perry, scratching behind his ears.

He must've heard the break in my voice, because he rested his chin heavily on my shoulder, and huffed his sweet hay breath into my hair.

'Ah, the dear boy, he's giving you a horse hug,' Lena observed.

It did feel that way. I'd never known a creature as gentle and sensitive as Perry. If a horse could count as a best friend, then he was certainly one of mine.

'I'd take you with me if I could,' I whispered to him.

He nuzzled my cheek, which was now salty wet with tears.

'I won't ever forget you, boy. I promise I won't.'

I'd saved him a carrot for this moment, but he wouldn't eat it, instead keeping his chin on my shoulder until Ma Blackwell came to tell me that if I didn't get a move on I'd miss the bus.

I cried all the way to school. And again at break time when I realised I still had Perry's carrot in my pocket.

I'd been amazed how well Mr Blackwell was bearing up, but later that afternoon, when he returned from the sale, his eyes were raw from crying.

'It fair broke my heart, it did,' he confessed. 'They knew I was leaving them there. They followed me right to the gate.'

Hearing this had me in tears all over again.

*

With the horses gone, everything felt final. All day cartloads of our furniture had been taken from Combe Grange up to the new cottage at Marley's Head. At teatime, we left Combe Grange for good. I couldn't believe I'd never wake up in our bedroom again, or listen to the wireless of an evening in the cosy, cluttered parlour, or turn the handle on the front door, and walk into the lovely old hallway.

A Channel swimmer like Gertrude Ederle, I

reminded myself, would always be looking ahead. You kept your eyes on the horizon, and instead of thinking of all the miles behind you, you focused on how incredible it was going to feel to arrive on dry land. More than that, Lena was with me. My lucky mascot. Everything, I told myself, was going to work out for the best.

*

The cottage at Marley's Head was indeed much, much smaller than Combe Grange. In my room there was only space for one narrow bed, so for the next couple of nights neither Lena nor I got much sleep. Late on Saturday a redirected letter arrived for Lena. She hurried upstairs to read it – she always liked to read her post alone – but not before I'd noticed the London postmark on the envelope. It was a reply from her father to the letter she'd written a few weeks ago. He'd never minded her staying on after her TB treatment, so I'd not given it much more thought. Now, though, I felt surprisingly nervous, and waited anxiously at the foot of the stairs.

'Well?' I demanded when she reappeared. 'Will he let you stay? Can you come on the boat?'

'Yes, and yes,' she replied. Yet I didn't think I'd imagined the hesitation before she smiled.

*

On Sunday morning, St Mary's held its final church service. The churchyard was heaving with people who'd come back to the village specially: most of them I recognised, like Mr Barnes the butcher, Neville the sheep farmer, Captain Farley, Mrs Lee, Jim, Maudie, Bill, Miss Setherton. Even Nate and his family had braved the crowds. It surprised me how some of the locals already looked more like town people, with new hairdos and smart shoes that would've never managed Syndercombe's muddy lanes. At least the churchyard had been tidied up since I was last here, though most of the headstones had gone, and there wasn't a yellow rose in sight.

Lena, I'd become increasingly aware, was out of sorts. I hoped it was mostly down to our rubbish sleeping arrangements, though I'd a feeling her father's letter was the more likely reason.

'Say, are you all right?' I whispered as we squeezed into the church. 'You've been glum since your dad's letter came.'

'Have I? I'm tip-top, honest.'

I wasn't convinced. Once we'd taken our seats inside, I couldn't even nudge her into a sly game of Mamas and Papas which would've helped pass the time. The service, thankfully, was relatively short. Poor Reverend Matthews tried to keep things joyful, with hymns and readings more suited to a wedding or a christening. But when the sun came streaming in through the beautiful stained-glass windows, his voice cracked.

'Forgive me,' he said, getting out his hanky.

It set off everyone else, and the church was suddenly a sea of white handkerchiefs, as if we were waving off an ocean liner, not a vicar and his church.

Abruptly, Lena stood up.

'Blow this for a lark,' she said under her breath, and, squeezing past everyone on our pew, went outside.

Something clearly *was* the matter, and ignoring Ma Blackwell's glares, I followed her into the churchyard, where I found Lena re-reading her father's letter. When she saw me coming, she folded it up. She was wearing a dress without pockets, so kept folding the letter, over and over, until it was small enough to hide inside her hands.

'You won't have a letter left at that rate,' I joked, but it fell flat. 'All right, out with it. What did your dad *really* say?

She winced. 'He says I've to come home tomorrow.'

'*Tomorrow?*' I stared at her in horror. 'But the swim's next week! Didn't you tell him you're on the pilot boat?'

'Course I did!' she cried. 'And before you say it, Nellie, I know how much you want me there. Believe me, I want to be there too.'

I didn't understand.

'Why can't you tell him you'll be back *after* the swim? It's only a few more days.'

'He says he's got this big surprise planned, just for me, and it can't wait. He's told Ma Blackwell. And . . .' As she opened her hands, the folded paper pinged apart, '. . . look what he sent, paid for and everything.'

Tucked in the letter was a train ticket. Lena held it up so I could see the details: a third-class seat on the ten o'clock train to London Waterloo, dated Monday the sixteenth of June.

I couldn't believe it.

'You . . . you . . . can't!' I cried.

We'd got this close to the Channel swim – just a *week* until it was due to happen – and now Lena's father, who'd not minded her staying on at Ma Blackwell's this past year, was suddenly expecting her home.

'Why so sudden?' I demanded, my frustration rising. 'What's the big rush for you to be back in London?'

'I don't know.' Lena was fighting back tears. 'I mean, I love Baapu, but I want to be with you . . . Oh, Nellie, what are we going to do?'

I tried to think. 'Well, I can't come with you to London, not this close to the swim, so—'

'We could run away, though, couldn't we, just for a few nights?' she cut in.

I thought she was joking. And I was about to say so when the church bells began ringing and it was suddenly too noisy to be heard. People had started leaving the church, standing in clusters on the path, or walking down to the White Lion where cider and sherry were being served on the pavement outside.

'We've got to do something,' I agreed, feeling hot and flustered. Then I spotted Nate. 'And we'll need to tell *him*.'

Clearly glad of an excuse to get away from his parents, Nate hurried over to us before I'd even tried to attract his attention.

'Morning, all. Everything okay?' he asked brightly.

'No,' I replied miserably. 'We've got a problem.'

On finding a quieter spot with fewer people and less bell-ringing, I explained about the letter and the ticket. Lena stayed stony-faced and silent until I'd finished. Then, again, she mentioned running away.

'Where, though?' I asked, a bit baffled as to why she thought it might work. 'We're setting off from here with the captain for the drive to Dover next Sunday.

What would we tell him?'

Nate cleared his throat. 'Speaking as someone who *has* run away, you need two things: somewhere to go, and money.'

All I had in my piggy bank was two shillings and a spare pyjama button. And I was pretty sure Lena didn't have any secret funds stashed away.

'I could lend you some dosh, if you like,' offered Nate.

I glanced at Lena, who was looking interested.

'But where would we go?' I pressed.

'Brighton,' Lena said, and quite boldly too. 'It's on the way to Dover – sort of. I've got an aunt who lives there. She's always wanted me to visit.'

'And the captain?'

'We'll send him a note.' Her mind, now it was on to something, was working whippet-fast. 'We'll ask the captain to pick us up from Brighton on Sunday, telling him we're going there to squeeze in some last-minute sea training—'

'While staying with your *beloved* aunt,' Nate added.

Lena smiled weakly. 'I hardly know her, to be honest.'

'But it sounds better if you do,' insisted Nate. 'Also, the Blackwells: it's best if we pretend they already know you've gone to Brighton.'

'But they won't know, will they?' I admitted guiltily.

'And they might worry and get in touch with the captain themselves.'

'Well, if they do he can put them straight, and they'll stop worrying—'

'Yeah, and be furious instead.'

I didn't know what to think, to be honest: but I couldn't bear for Lena to go home. If I stood the remotest chance of swimming the Channel I needed her there, not to mention the life we'd promised ourselves once this was all over.

'Okay,' I said, rather shakily. 'Let's give it a go.'

Lena hugged me. Nate agreed to lend us five pounds, which would more than cover two train tickets to Brighton. What I wasn't expecting was him to ask if he could come with us.

'Why not, old thing?'

'Well . . .' I spluttered. 'Your parents, to start with.'

The Clatworthys were the sort who'd kick up a massive stink and get the police on to us straight away. It might well blow our entire plan.

'Not if we're keeping the captain informed,' Nate reasoned. 'At least then the grown-ups won't panic.'

'Ha! Won't they?' I wasn't so sure, but Nate kept on.

'Really, Nellie, it's because of you and Lena that I've not been marched straight back to school. You're two of the finest chums I've ever had, so whatever it is you're doing, so am I. I'm part of this, remember?'

I chewed my bottom lip, thinking over what he said. The captain, Mrs Lamb, Nate's parents, the Channel Swimming officials all expected the swimmer on the sixteenth of June to be Nate himself. Part of the reason why it wouldn't be was me: I wanted this swim more than he did. I wanted it more than pretty much anything, and he was giving me my dream. So it felt quite shabby to not include him. We'd be better off facing the next few days together.

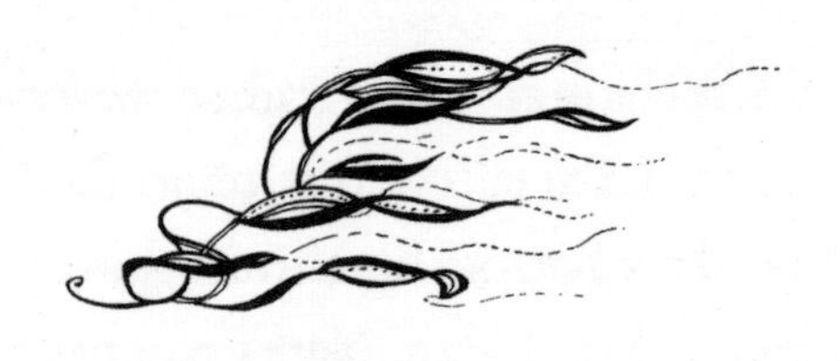

19.
EARLY SUMMER, 1952
NELLIE

On Monday morning, we had bacon and eggs for our farewell-to-Lena breakfast. I was almost too excited to eat. Ma Blackwell supposed this unusual turn of events was because I was upset at Lena leaving, and told me to buck up.

'I'm making your favourite for tea,' she also said, in a softer voice. 'Suet pudding and custard,' which made me feel awful that I wouldn't be here to eat it. She'd find out soon enough, though, when Captain Farley got our letter in the afternoon post. Plus, I'd only be gone a few days.

It had already been agreed I could go with Lena as far as the station before heading into school. The train to Brighton was the same one as the ten o'clock to London, only we'd get off earlier to change trains at Clapham

Junction. Nate was meeting us at the bus stop on the main road.

At nine o'clock, I donned my school bag – swimming costume and hat stowed inside – and fetched my coat. Lena shrugged on her own, picked up her suitcase, and we all followed her outside to the gate. I stood aside, nervous, as Lena said her goodbyes to the Blackwells.

'You're a strong, healthy girl now,' Ma Blackwell told her, holding her by the elbows and peering into her face. 'So go well, d'you hear me?'

Lena smiled her warmest smile. 'Ta for everything, Ma Blackwell. And to you, Mr Blackwell. I've loved living at Combe Grange.'

Mr Blackwell was brimful of tears yet again. I couldn't bear it, and went to hug him, but Lena steered me towards the gate.

'Don't! You'll make it worse!' she whispered.

We stepped out on to the road. The gate clicked shut behind us. A quick glance over my shoulder confirmed the Blackwells were heading back indoors. Linking arms, we set off down the road. Since Nate's timekeeping wasn't his strong point, it was a relief to find him already at the bus stop. He looked bigger than normal, like he was wearing four coats all at once.

'Morning, all!' he greeted us exuberantly.

'Blimey, how much clothing have you got on?' asked Lena.

'Just a couple of extra sweaters.' He pulled up a trouser leg. 'And my pyjamas. Couldn't be seen packing a suitcase, could I?'

I burst out laughing. It *was* funny, and it helped relax us a bit as we waited.

'I've got sandwiches too, in case anyone's hungry.' Nate patted his school satchel, which was so full he'd not been able to buckle the straps.

'Didn't your parents wonder why you were making so much lunch?' I asked, genuinely amazed, because at ours you couldn't eat a single currant without Ma Blackwell noticing.

'Told them it was for after training,' he answered proudly.

Lena glanced at her watch. There was no sign of the bus yet.

'It should've been here by now,' she muttered, looking up and down the road.

'It'll be the army roadblocks holding everything up,' Nate remarked. 'I had to cut across the fields. Went past the back of your old house, as it happens.'

'Oh.' I felt a pang of sadness. All too vividly I could picture Combe Grange's empty rooms and outside, the quiet stable yard, and Lena's beautifully polished front door. I dearly wished I'd taken something from the house as a keepsake – a stone from the orchard wall, a window catch, that lovely brass door handle. It was too late now.

Lena, meanwhile, was growing more impatient. 'Geez, where *is* that bus?'

Normally, the town bus climbed the valley via a road that skirted Syndercombe. That road was visible from the field opposite, so I crossed over and climbed the gate to see if there was any approaching traffic: there wasn't. The road was silent. In total contrast, the village was buzzing with activity.

The deadline had passed at two this morning: the village was now officially uninhabited, so I'd expected it to look empty. Yet there were people down there, as small as ants, running between the houses. And the main street, from church to post office, was blocked with army vehicles.

'You know they're using explosives left over from the war?' Nate said, joining me to watch.

'What on earth for?'

'To flatten the buildings, apparently. Makes it less eerie, I suppose, when they flood the valley.'

'Really?' I was shocked. 'I think it makes it ten times worse.'

A group had gathered on the other side of the river. From the village side, an army man was waving his arms, as if telling them to keep back. Three other soldiers ran out of a nearby house. It was the last on the street – *our* old house, I realised, stiffening.

'Oh no!' I cried. 'That's Combe—'

The explosion blew me backwards. I landed in the middle of the road, surrounded by soil and stones and chunks of white and pink body parts, I was sure of it. I'd scraped my knee and my ears were ringing but, miraculously, I was still in one piece. The pink and white chunks, I saw now, were Nate's spam sandwiches, strewn across the road. A plume of smoke wafted upwards from the village.

A few yards away, Nate was helping Lena, who'd been thrown against the hedge.

'Are you okay?' I called, getting up.

'Alive, thanks,' Nate replied. 'Can't say the same about my sandwiches.'

Dusting ourselves off, we regrouped by the bus stop. I could feel my knees shaking, and tried my hardest not to think of Combe Grange reduced to a pile of rubble. Lena put a comforting arm around my shoulders.

Just when we'd almost given up hope of making the ten o'clock train, our bus appeared. It was, by Lena's watch, twenty minutes late. Amazingly, it had avoided the village blast entirely. They'd come the coast way, the driver told us, though he was horrified to hear how close he'd been to driving into the middle of the explosion.

'Glad I was running late, then,' he confessed.

We clearly looked a bit of a state because, as we climbed on board, the entire bus fell silent. A couple of ladies asked if we were all right.

'Perfectly, thank you,' Nate smiled, all politeness.

Once we'd sat down, the other passengers started chatting again – about everything from the price of cabbages to whether Errol Flynn the actor was married. Lena's fingers tapped impatiently against her suitcase.

'Come on, come on,' she muttered.

'We'll get there, don't worry,' I said, trying to stay calm.

It was now quarter to ten.

Lena checked her watch. And checked it again. It was becoming harder not to be alarmed. The bus was pulling in at every stop on the main road. People got on and off. Money rattled on the counter, the driver chatted, tickets were handed out. Everything seemed to take for ever. Even the bus itself, when it finally swerved out into the traffic, caught every red traffic light, every pedestrian crossing.

We were already on our feet as the bus swung into the station. We ran into the entrance hall. Infuriatingly, there was a queue at the ticket booth.

'I expect we can buy tickets on the train,' Nate assured us.

Our platform was reached through another door across the hall, beyond which came the squeal of brakes. The train we needed to catch was pulling into the station. We'd make it if we kept running. Lena, though, stopped dead in her tracks.

'Oh!' I tumbled into her, banging my scraped knee on her suitcase. 'What're you—?'

I looked up. Just ahead of us was a man, tall, wearing a suit and a dark blue turban, and a woman in a tunic and trousers. Lena breathed in sharply. She was staring at the couple – just as the man and woman were gazing directly at her – in such a burning, tender way that made it obvious they all knew each other.

'Lena,' I said, confused. 'What's going on?'

Lena put down her suitcase.

'I'm sorry,' she whispered to me, to Nate, not taking her eyes off the woman who was now coming towards her. 'It's Mata. I'd no idea she'd be here!'

If it had been Ma Blackwell standing there, having got wind of our plan, it would've made more sense. Or the Clatworthys. Or Captain Farley.

But Lena's mother and father? Her dad lived in

London, didn't he, and her mum was still in India? They couldn't be *here*.

'If we turn round and run,' I hissed, 'we can hide out till later, then catch another train.'

'Good plan.' Nate reached down to pick up Lena's suitcase, but she pushed his hand away.

'I'm sorry,' she said again.

My throat tightened with panic. This wasn't meant to happen.

'Le-Le?' the woman said. 'Come! We must hurry for our train!'

I didn't understand. Lena couldn't leave me. I'd go to London with her if she asked, or India. I'd even forget all about the Channel swim.

But Lena didn't ask.

The woman who was her mother held out her hand and Lena took it. Laughing, shaking her head, staring at Lena in utter amazement, she led her away from us towards the platform. Bit by bit I broke into tiny pieces because I knew this was goodbye. This was the big surprise her father had been planning. We wouldn't be going to Brighton. Lena wasn't coming on the pilot boat. Her parents were here to take her home.

Yet in the doorway, Lena hesitated, and I thought,

for a second, she'd changed her mind, that she wasn't leaving after all.

'Nellie, I'm sorry,' she said. 'I'll write to you. I'll follow it in the newspapers. Just promise me you'll do the—'

'Come, Le-Le,' her mother hurried her on. 'The train will not wait for us.'

And she was gone. I stared after her, bewildered. On the platform, the guard's whistle shrieked as the last of the train doors slammed shut.

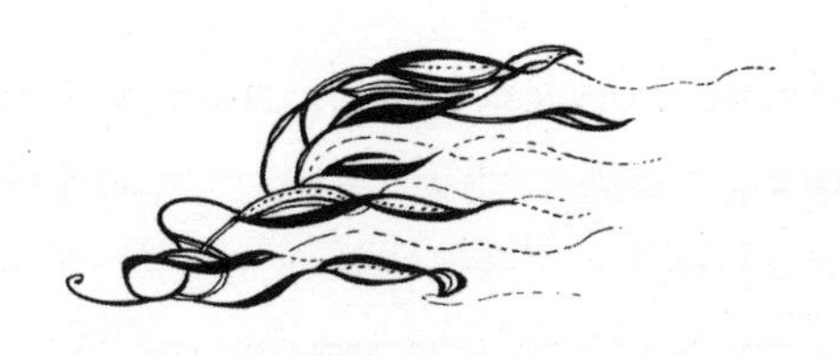

20.
SUMMER, 2032
POLLY

I crawl out of the lake, gasping. I don't know what to feel: relief? Shock? I'm glad I'm on my own this time, so I can sit on the ground, head in hands, and think.

So Lena and Nellie don't run away.

I'm completely thrown. Part of me is thinking of Joel's big secret, the relief that he didn't run away that night I caught him on the balcony, yet for Lena and Nellie this doesn't feel right. After all their plans and promises, I'd assumed they'd be the one part of the story that *did* work out. And to think they were coming to Brighton – my home town! But it didn't happen. It went wrong. Which goes to show that even the strongest friendships can break.

Back at the house I can't sleep. The air feels tight, prickly. I turn the pillow over, push back the sheet, pull it up again. It's hopeless trying to rest when my brain keeps churning, stirring, whirling like a machine.

Mary Foster.

I sit up. Now my heart's racing too. Mary Foster, the name on Nellie's mother's gravestone. Okay, so in those days, Mary was probably a common enough name, but I can't help thinking these two Marys are linked. The Mary up the lane can't be Nellie's mum, because she's already dead. But I've a feeling she's *someone* in all of this. I just need to find out who.

*

The next morning the sky is heavy and grey. At breakfast, just the effort of lifting our cereal spoons is enough to make us sweat. Jessie's complaining of a headache.

'Too much to do, *way* too much to do,' she mutters, as her device keeps dinging with notifications. One message makes her particularly frustrated. 'Oh great, just what I need.'

'What is?' I ask.

She turns her screen to show me the news report. A big storm is coming up from France, crossing the English Channel, and due to hit us later this evening or early tomorrow.

'Rain, huh?' Joel raises his eyebrows. 'Sounds exciting.'

'Not a joke, matey,' she replies. 'It's a nasty-looking storm.'

Her screen shows weather warnings, flood warnings, a whole list of red triangles. There's a chance of power cuts, floods, fallen trees, blocked train lines and afterwards, food shortages that could go on for days. It's not uncommon for the weather to wreak havoc, though this storm does sound a particularly bad one. We're told to expect record rainfall, and to avoid all travel after six o'clock tonight.

Even time travel? I wonder. Not that it would stop me: I'm going to the lake tonight, no matter what the weather's doing.

'There's real concern that even major roads will become impassable,' says the weather forecaster in an online clip.

'Fingers crossed we can't get back in time to start school,' Joel says.

'Huh! I wish.' I'm feeling particularly sore about Sasha this morning, so the thought is very appealing.

Yet before we get our hopes up, Dad calls. Jessie puts him on loudspeaker as she starts to gather her things for work.

'Kids? You've seen the weather, right?' he says.

'Yeah, Dad,' Joel replies. 'It's going to rain. A lot.'

'A heck of a lot, so I'm coming to pick you up early, while I can still get through. I should be there about one o'clock, okay?' Dad sounds as if he's in the van, already on the road.

'*Today?*' I'm horrified.

Joel puts his earphones back in and gets up from the table. But I'm panicking – and not just because if we go back to Brighton my brother might do something stupid and take off to London. Going home early means I'll never find out what happens to Nellie or Lena, or if the Channel swim-swap actually takes place.

'Not today, Dad!' I cry.

'Sorry, Pol. I don't want your mum worrying.'

'We're fine here. We'll be safe with Jessie.'

Dad sighs. 'Sorry, pet. I know you're having a fab time.'

It's far more than that. It's the threads of Nellie's story still hanging in the air: it feels so tied to us, tied to Joel and me and that stupid night on the beach. If we go home now, he'll run away: I'm really scared he will. Nate said that to properly run away you needed money and a place to go, and Joel doesn't have either of those. If I can go back to Nellie's life one more time, I might at least understand how things end, and what I can do to help my brother.

I look pleadingly at Jessie, hoping she'll back me up, but she pulls a sad face.

'If this storm's as bad as they say it's going to be, then it's sensible, petal,' she reasons.

Dad hangs up. All I can do is go and pack my stuff, and try not to cry, though the tears are welling up. To have come so far with Nellie only for it to end like this is crushing. It makes me think of that day at the station, when she was all geared up for an adventure, and instead had to lose her best friend.

I'm sitting on my bed when Jessie knocks and sticks her head in.

'Could you do me a quick favour?' She holds out a white paper bag, the sort you get from a pharmacy. 'These are for Mary. More blood pressure tablets. Would you mind dropping them in? I'm run off my feet this morning what with the storm coming.'

Jessie sees my surprise. 'I know I told you to keep away. But she does need these, and I'd be really grateful.'

'Sure.' I take the bag.

It's then I see Mary's full name: it's on the printed label stuck to the bag. 'Mary Elizabeth Foster – DOB 07/01/1941.'

'You okay, petal?' Jessie wants to know.

I look up, dizzily. 'Yeah, fine. I'll take these up to her now.'

I grab my sandals, tugging them on without undoing

the buckles. It's not the homework task I'm thinking of. It's so much more – *too* much, almost. My heart's roaring in my chest.

Foster is Nellie's surname. The date of birth – 1941– would make Mary the exact same age as Nellie in 1952. It's all falling into place: Shakespeare Cottage, Mary's knowledge of Channel swimming. Even the middle name is right: there's a girl in my class called Nell and she told me it's short for Elizabeth.

I make sure I take the old door handle with me: I've a feeling it's going to help. I'm in full flight out of the door when Joel calls me back.

'You got a sec, Pol?'

He's in his room, looking at his screen. My stomach sinks when I see it's open on the site where that swimming clip got posted. He's scrolling through the comments: there's more of them than ever. I wish he'd stop going back to it, going over it, torturing himself – and me. Yet there's something about the way Joel looks that's almost *defiant*.

'You asked me to check out Sasha's accounts, yeah?'

I nod uneasily.

'Well, she didn't block you.'

'Oh.' Somehow, this is a relief. 'Okay.'

'But I've found out who filmed us,' he says. 'I think

they're the same person who put the clip online.'

I perch next to him on the bed, suddenly nervous. There's something in the way he says it that makes me want to know – and not know – who it is. He doesn't say the name out loud. He does what Jessie did with the news, and turns his screen towards me so I can see it for myself. The page is so full of messages and images, I'm not sure where to look until Joel, finger hovering, directs my eyes to the right place.

SASHA_TORTE20

My blood runs cold. I know the username. Sasha explained the pun to me one Saturday afternoon, taking me past a cake shop in town and pointing out a glossy chocolate cake in the window.

'That.' She tapped the glass with a stubby fingernail. 'Is my favourite thing in the world. A Sachertorte.'

It's typical of Sasha to name herself after a cake. All her accounts have the same name, more or less. Yet it's not like her to be deliberately nasty – thoughtless, yes, but not cruel. And would she really be on the old pier in the middle of the night?

Some of the comments posted under the clip are so vile I feel sick reading them. Would Sasha – my often silly, bit-of-a-joker friend – think it was okay to film someone and post it online without asking? And since when did she hate my brother so much to do this to him? To me?

'Sasha wouldn't post that clip,' I say.

Wouldn't she? says another voice. Why else has she not been in touch? Why've all her media accounts closed down apart from this one?

I don't know. It feels as if the storm is already here, inside my head. Yet Joel looks brighter than he has done for days, maybe weeks. He's on a trail that should lead him to who's been making his life hell at school.

'We're getting somewhere,' he says.

Maybe. I stand up, push my hair off my hot face. But one mystery at a time.

21.
SUMMER, 2032
POLLY

Mary answers her door surprisingly quickly. She's wearing a pink jumper and matching knitted gloves. She looks tired.

'Yes, dear?'

'Hello, Mary, it's Polly. I've brought your tablets.' I'm doing my best to be cheery and friendly, when really I'm dying to get straight to the point.

She looks at me. At the pharmacy bag.

'I met you the other day when my aunt Jessie and I brought you home?' I try.

My heart sinks as I see the confusion in her face. She doesn't recognise me, or Jessie's name.

'I'm sorry . . . I don't take . . . who are you? What do you want?' she says.

'No, please, it's all right.' I'm muddling her, and

that's the last thing I want to do. 'You told me about swimming, about Shakespeare Beach.'

She wracks her brain for the memory, then, when she finds it, suddenly lights up.

'Polly!' she cries. 'Of course! Jessie's niece! Why didn't you say so?'

And she invites me in.

The cottage is only slightly cooler than outside. As we edge along the hallway, past the bin bags, I'm certain this old woman *is* Nellie. I feel it in my bones. It's not just about the date of birth or the name: it's the sense I've met her before. Not that she looks like younger Nellie: she's small, bone-thin, with white hair tied back in a tortoiseshell clip. But her voice, the way it goes up at the end, and her eyes – steady, level – are so familiar. It's as if I've known her for years.

'My legs aren't what they used to be,' Mary says. 'Shall we sit down?'

We go into the sitting room, and amongst the thermal vests and newspapers locate a pair of armchairs. Though the curtains are open, the room is so dim Mary switches on a lamp. I sit on the edge of my chair, trying not to be too eager.

'I should offer you some tea,' Mary says. 'But I haven't

seen the kettle since Monday. It's getting a bit much these days, living here.'

I nod. All I can think is: *she's Nellie!* But sharing my time-travel experience might be a bit much straight off, so I keep going with the polite chit-chat.

'Have you talked to Jessie about moving?' I ask. 'She says there are some nice places where you can get the help you need.'

Mary gives me a killer glare. 'You're a bold one, aren't you?'

'Oh. Umm . . . Sorry.' I've said the wrong thing. 'It's none of my business. Everyone in my family thinks I talk too much when I'd be better keeping quiet.'

'And I've a reputation for being stubborn and set in my ways, so there we are,' she replies. 'So . . .'

'Polly,' I remind her.

'Polly. Are you staying long with your aunt?'

'I'm going home today because of the storm. My mum's worried about us – she's having a baby, or will be in a few months. It's a bit of a surprise, actually. Jessie thinks there are too many people on the planet already.'

'Babies, eh? They do complicate things, that's what my mother used to say.'

'Did she? Why?'

'Oh, you know.' She wafts her hand vaguely. 'So you're going home today, eh? By train?'

Grown-ups always like discussing journeys; I've no idea why.

'My dad's on his way,' I say. 'Though our van's quite old so it'll probably take him ages to get here.'

'Where's he coming from?'

I pause: now *this* should be interesting.

'Brighton,' I tell her. 'It's where we live, right on the seafront.'

I watch her reaction: she frowns, mulls it over, taps the arms of the chair with her fingers.

'I've always wanted to go to Brighton,' she says, with a sad sigh. Then her eyes are back on me. 'Are you a swimmer?'

'Not really. I mean, I can stay afloat, but I'm not that good at it.' I steer the question back to Mary: it's her I want to know about. 'Why, are *you*?'

'Oh, dear me!' She laughs. 'It's hard to imagine it, isn't it? But I was a swimmer, yes, a long time ago, and I was quite good at it, as it happens.'

I shut my eyes for a second. Breathe deep. Open my eyes again. She IS Nellie Foster. I'm so happy I want to hug her, but that would probably freak her out.

'Where did you swim?' Though I know the

answer, I'm desperate to keep her talking. 'In Truthwater Lake?'

Mary rolls her eyes. 'I expect Jessie's told you the story, has she?'

Not Jessie, I think. *You*, Mary, you've told me the story.

Mary covers her mouth as she yawns. 'Excuse me. I've had awful trouble sleeping these past few nights.'

'It's been really hot.'

'It's not the heat. I've been waking up, bang on two o'clock in the morning for some reason. It's very odd.'

It's not odd to me. I know exactly why she's been waking up at that time. Unable to hold back any longer, I take the plunge.

'You're called Nellie, really, aren't you? Or you were when you were a girl.'

She blinks. 'Good gracious! It's years since anyone's called me that.'

But she remembers, all right. Encouraged, I keep going.

'Why did you stop swimming if you were good at it?' I ask.

Now she looks confused.

'You were training to swim the English Channel with a boy called Nate, who got picked by the selectors but didn't want to do it,' I remind her.

'The Channel? Did I say that?'

'Lena, then,' I try instead. 'She was your best friend, wasn't she? But then she went back to London with her father.'

I'm saying too much. I'm overwhelming her.

'Why are you asking me this?' Mary scowls. 'Is this some sort of test? Did Jessie send you here to prove I can't remember things properly?'

'No, of course she didn't!'

Mary folds her arms. She's silent. And so am I, frustrated and worried that I've blown my one chance to hear the end of Nellie's story. As I shift in my seat, something knocks uncomfortably against my hipbone. It's the old door handle. I'd brought it with me in the hope Mary might remember it. Surely it's worth a try.

It's jammed deep in my pocket, but with a tug and a grunt I pull it out.

'Do you recognise this?' I ask, holding it towards her.

Mary keeps her eyes on me. She's not willing to look at what I'm showing her. I wait, trying my best to be patient, holding the handle in my palm until my arm starts to ache. Still, I don't move. And eventually, her eyes flicker from my face to my hand. It's the quickest of looks – a swoop. A glance.

'Combe Grange! Oh, sweet heavens!' she gasps. 'Where did you get *that*?'

As she takes it from me, the handle clicks open, and Nellie, smiling, begins to remember.

'I always regretted not taking this as a keepsake,' she says. 'I might be old, but it all still feels like yesterday.'

I don't ask her anything else. I don't need to go swimming or time travelling. Nellie Foster is here, alive, sitting in front of me, and what better way to find out what happened than from the person whose story it is. All I have to do now is listen. And for a talker like me that's challenge enough, but I'm ready for it.

22.
SUMMER, 1952
NELLIE

When Lena left it was like losing Mam all over again. I kept expecting to see her, only instead to be faced with the space she'd left behind. I missed having her to talk to. There was no one who listened like she did, no one else I'd want to share everything with. I couldn't imagine talking so freely to anyone ever again.

As for the swim, what was the point in chasing sponsorship money I no longer needed? The plan was stupid, anyway, thinking Nate and I could swap places. I was ready to give up on the whole idea.

That first day without Lena, Ma Blackwell was kind. It was natural to miss her, she said, when we'd been like two peas in a pod. But by Wednesday she'd had enough of my moping, and with Mr Blackwell – and Mam's headstone – took me on the bus to the new cemetery where my mother was now buried. There were acres of graves in every direction, with pathways to walk along and benches on which to sit. The graves moved from St Mary's formed a freshly dug row at the cemetery's furthest edge. Mr Blackwell, who'd brought his spade, made a trench for the headstone which Ma Blackwell and I then eased into place.

'There,' said Ma Blackwell afterwards. 'Don't that look grand?'

Mr Blackwell stood aside so I could have a proper look. The headstone was as pristine as ever – no chips, no scratches; we'd made sure of that. Yet in such a big, open graveyard it looked smaller and plainer, somehow. A bunch of yellow roses would've helped.

Ma Blackwell took me firmly by the shoulders.

'Now then, Nellie, we've all lost people,' she said. 'But you need to make a fresh start – new house, new school, and you've still got next week on the boat to look forward to.'

I cried then, thinking she didn't understand.

'*You* know how it feels,' I sobbed, turning to Mr Blackwell. 'You had to give up Perry and Sage.'

His eyes misted over. 'Aye, but it comforts me knowing they're getting fat on Devon grass and living the life of kings. Tis no good dwelling on the past when there's a big, bright future out there.'

I'd never had Mr Blackwell as the optimistic type, and his answer didn't help.

*

Then there was Nate. He too was patient at first. Yet when he asked me why I'd missed Thursday's training session, we both lost our tempers.

'It's all off then, is it?' Nate demanded. 'We'll tell the swimming people? Forget the whole thing?'

'*You* could do the swim.' I was being difficult: we both knew he wasn't up to it.

'And this is all because of Lena leaving?'

'Course it is!' I cried. Crikey, he was stupid sometimes. 'You know why I was doing it.'

'For the money? *Only* the money?'

'Easy for you to say,' I shot back. 'You've never been poor.'

'I've never wanted to swim the English Channel, either, or had an incredible talent that would make me the best of my age in the whole world.'

'You only want me to do it so you don't have to,' I muttered.

'At first, maybe,' he admitted. 'But you know where

I'd be now if it wasn't for you, don't you? I'd be back at prep school, totally and utterly miserable, even if it is the last week of term.'

'Then you should know how I'm feeling without Lena,' I replied.

'Geez! Lena's not the only person on the planet! *I'm* your friend too, you know!'

I glared at him.

'Look, I know how driven you are,' Nate went on. 'You'll regret it if you give up this chance.'

'But I don't care about the sponsorship any more,' I argued.

'Nellie.' He grew very stern. 'You know there's more at stake here – far, far more.'

'Is there?'

But deep down I understood what he was telling me. I'd wanted to swim the English Channel long before I met Lena. Mam had told me not to be ordinary. Lena said she'd follow the swim story in the news. There were plenty of good reasons not to give up now.

Though it was hard to think of a future without Lena or Mam in it, if I did this, and succeeded, I'd be the first child in the world to swim all the way to France. If the officials didn't like it, if Nate's dad was furious, then I'd still have proved myself. And who knew what exciting possibilities might come next? After all I'd lost – mother, best friend, home – the swim was the one thing giving me hope that dreams really could come true.

The fight in me hadn't gone anywhere, I realised then. I was still me, still a swimmer, still as stubborn as anything.

'All right, I get it. I'm doing this for me,' I said.

Nate gave a huge sigh of relief. 'Glad to hear it, old thing! France is rather splendid in June, you know.'

'You've been?'

'Twice, actually.'

Of course he had: I rolled my eyes at him, laughing.

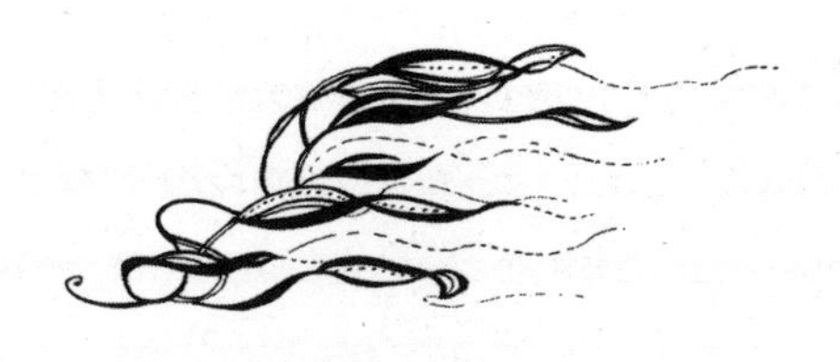

23.
SUMMER, 1952
NELLIE

Suddenly, it was Sunday. The morning before the swim dawned a dazzling, rose-petal red. I'd been allowed a few days off school to 'accompany Nate' so refused to believe the sky was a bad omen, despite the old saying. It was incredible to think we'd got this far, even if it was without Lena. Nate's prep school term had officially finished so he was, in theory, safe. Even when our ruse was discovered, he wouldn't be sent back there. The big challenge now was swapping places on the boat. We'd be in trouble with the officials, we accepted that part of it all. We just had to make sure no one stopped the swim before I got to France. People could say what they liked afterwards: it wouldn't matter once I'd broken a world record.

'Be outside at seven o'clock sharp,' Captain Farley warned. 'Punctuality wins the day.'

We were driving the two hundred and fifty miles to Dover in his car. I was ready a whole two hours early.

'They'll have life jackets on the boat, won't they? The captain will keep an eye on you?' Ma Blackwell said, looking as nervous as I felt.

'I can swim,' I assured her, adding quickly, 'If I have to.'

'So could people on the *Titanic*,' she answered darkly.

All through breakfast, my nerves increased. I kept checking the window and pacing about the kitchen. When Captain Farley finally arrived Nate was already in the car and in a similarly jumpy mood. His family were setting off for France on the ferry later that morning to cheer him on when he reached Cap Gris-Nez.

Though, of course, if our plan worked, it would be *me* walking out of the sea, not Nate. I didn't want to think about how his family would react. In helping me he was disappointing them, that was the truth of it. At very best it was going to be painfully awkward.

'If my father's disappointed, so what? He's *always* been disappointed in me,' was Nate's response. 'I escaped going back to prep school, and made two glorious chums. I'd say I've done very nicely out of our arrangement, thank you.'

Maybe.

Personally, I thought Nate was being remarkably

brave. I'd have loved to have someone there on the beach in France, waiting for me to come ashore. More than that, I wished Lena was here with us. But I had to accept that she wasn't, and I could still do this without her.

Thankfully, Captain Farley's car was noisy enough for us to talk in whispers and not be heard. Against the drone of the engine and the rumble of the tyres, we went over the finer details of what we were planning. The pilot boat would leave Dover harbour at two in the morning with us on board, then Nate would be dropped by Shakespeare Beach to start his swim from the official point.

'I'll have my costume on under my sweater,' I reminded Nate. 'And when you're about to go in, I'll distract them—'

'By shouting "buoy" in the water!'

'And when they turn round, I'll jump in—'

'And by the time they notice it's you not me it'll be too late because you can't touch a swimmer once they're in the water.'

It was a flimsy plan, and talking it through again didn't exactly fill me with confidence. But it was too late to change it now.

Then, as we neared Salisbury Plain, Captain Farley dropped a bombshell.

'You've heard about the film crew, yes?' he asked, watching for our reactions in the mirror. 'Mr Wrigley's chartered his own boat. They'll be following us to film the entire swim.'

Nate and I looked at each other, horrified.

'A *film crew*? Cripes alive!' gasped Nate.

I felt suddenly ill. Our entire plan rested on the pilot boat's crew not paying proper attention, but this meant even more pairs of eyes on us, more torches lighting up the dark. Even if we did manage to swap, the whole escapade, including Nate's family's reactions, would be caught on film, for ever. I slumped into my seat, defeated. If Lena was here she'd know what to do. But she wasn't, and Nate, I sensed, was looking to me for answers that I didn't have.

*

By the time we reached Dover, I'd recovered a little. If we stuck to our plan then we *could* do this. We just had to hold our nerve for a few more hours. But at the hotel, we were met by a room full of cameras and reporters, and I was terrified all over again.

'They're here for us, aren't they?' I croaked.

'I believe so,' Captain Farley replied, glowering.

'Though I'd hoped we might catch our breath before the press conference.'

Mrs Lamb, immaculate as ever in suit and pearls, ushered us into the hotel's ballroom and to a raised area at the front. There we sat, facing a frighteningly large audience. My shoes needed a polish, I realised. I'd dropped butter on my skirt. Worse of all was that Nate and I were lying to everyone, and couldn't back out now, even if we'd wanted to. Like me, the captain was uncomfortable with all the attention. Nate was the complete opposite, smiling pleasantly, sitting easily in his seat.

One by one the reporters put their questions:

'Sam Patel, *Dover Mercury*. You Channel swimmers are the new movie stars. How does it feel being part of the latest craze?'

And:

'Cynthia Bloom, *London Evening Herald*. What's the first thing you plan to do when you reach France?'

Then:

'Scott Kauffman, *Washington Post*. When are you coming to America, Nate? I hear President Truman is very keen to meet you.'

The *president*?

I'd never felt so out of my depth in my life. Yet

Nate took it all in his stride, and spoke to the reporters as if they were old friends. Would they still be chummy towards us when they realised they'd been duped, I wondered? Would Mr Wrigley cancel his sponsorship?

Thankfully, the press conference soon ended after that. We were then introduced to our pilot.

'Johnny Hawkins is the name,' he told us.

He wore a blue cap and old tweed coat that was freckled with sand and sea salt. I found the sight of him oddly reassuring.

'Are you missing one?' he asked, eyes skimming over us all. 'Wasn't there supposed to be another girl?'

The captain looked a bit baffled. 'I'm sorry?'

'Ah, never mind. Must've been a mistake.'

I was grateful he hadn't mentioned Lena by name.

'You're the swimmer, aren't you, lad?' he asked, turning to Nate. 'Ready for the challenge?'

Nate squared his shoulders, deliberately not looking at me. 'I am, Mr Hawkins.'

'Glad to hear it. Can't say I'm going to enjoy having a film crew following us – a lot of fuss and hoo-ha, if you ask me – but it's what Mr Wrigley's paying for.'

'Nate will be fine,' Captain Farley assured him. 'He simply needs a little—'

'Because your pal here,' the pilot interrupted, indicating me. 'She can swim alongside you for a wee while for support, if you need it.'

This was news to us.

'I can?' I cried.

Nate's entire face lit up. 'By jove, Nellie! What do you say to *that*?'

I seized the chance with both hands.

'We *do* need it. Definitely!' I insisted.

A swap in the water, at a safe distance from the captain and the pilot, would be far easier than swapping on board, right under their noses.

'You'll have to keep your distance,' Mr Hawkins cautioned us. 'No touching or the swim will be void. And only for a couple of hours, that's the rules.'

'Absolutely, Mr Hawkins,' Nate replied.

'You're a lucky lad to be allowed a support swimmer. Must've made a strong case in your application, eh?' the pilot mused.

Nate smiled politely, though we both knew it wasn't his doing. It was Lena's.

24.
SUMMER, 1952
NELLIE

What remained of the evening was spent in our hotel room. Nate lay on his bed, snoring: it amazed me that he could sleep at a time like this. The captain and I occupied a pair of armchairs under the window, both of us tense and quiet. My mind was whizzing. The pilot's suggestion was a help to us, yes, but once I was in the water and Nate was on the boat again, he'd have to pretend to be me until France. There was so much that could go wrong.

'Nellie, I've something for you,' the captain said, suddenly.

Taking a book from his pocket, he passed it to me. The book was old, leather-bound, with gold on the page edges like the special Bible Reverend Matthews used at weddings and Christmas. On the cover it said *Selected*

Poems by Christina Rossetti. I'd never heard of the book, and wasn't sure why he was giving it to me.

'It was your mother's favourite,' he explained, seeing my confusion.

I swallowed. 'Oh.'

'She'd often read in the library at Hadfield Hall. She'd sit in the window seat, you know, the one that gets the sun in the mornings?'

I knew the seat he meant, yes, but didn't know Mam liked poetry. Nor did I realise that she read the books she was paid to dust, or that Captain Farley didn't mind when she did. I felt caught out, somehow, that I should've known these things and didn't.

'Umm . . .' I mumbled. 'Thank you . . . errr . . . I suppose.'

'Yes, well.' Captain Farley looked awkward. 'I am also fully aware these past months have been testing for you.'

Testing? Did he mean Mam not being here, or being overlooked by Mrs Lamb, or the village flooding or Lena leaving? There was plenty to choose from, all told.

'I have been sad,' I admitted. 'Especially when Lena left. I thought she didn't want to go back to London, but I was wrong, wasn't I?'

The captain grew thoughtful. 'You know, sometimes there are reasons as to why a family can't be together. And if those reasons change, and the family *can* reunite again, then—'

'I am happy she's got her mum back,' I interrupted. 'Honestly, I am.'

'Ah, Nellie.' He smiled, softening. 'You've been a true friend to Lena – and to Nate, at a time when they both needed your friendship very much.'

'Actually, sir, I needed theirs too.'

'Indeed. Friends and family, eh? Where would we be without them?'

He fell quiet again. I'd not seen him like this before, softly spoken, dreamy. Nor had I ever heard him talk about Mam and poetry books and families.

'Your mother would be terribly proud of you, Nellie,' he said with a sigh.

'For the swimming?'

'For everything.'

It was the nicest thing I'd heard for ages. I hugged the book to my chest.

Behind us, on the bed, Nate was waking up. It was time to get ready. Bending over my bag, I put the poetry book away to read later when this was all over. As I did so, Captain Farley dropped his voice:

'Do what you have to do tonight.'

I froze, all the blood rushing to my face.

'Supporting Nate, d'you mean?' I asked, straightening stiffly.

The captain gave a tiny shake of his head.

'I know how much *you* want to do this, Nellie, and I know that Nate doesn't. You're going to swap places in order for you to swim the Channel – ah, let me finish!' he insisted, when I tried to interrupt.

'You'll be breaking the rules so you probably won't make the history books, but, if you succeed, if you keep going, if no one spots what's happened and pulls you out of the water, you'll still be the first child to swim to France.'

My heart was in my throat. He knew everything. So much for his noisy car engine: he must've heard us talking on the way here. Or did it start back at the gravel pits on the day he'd thought I was Nate? Maybe he'd always known I'd pull a stunt like this: I'd certainly had my suspicions.

'Don't look so terrified,' the captain said. 'Just stick to your plan and I'll do my very best to go along with it.'

I stared at him. He knew what we were doing, and was going to help us? I honestly didn't know what to say.

Behind us, the bed creaked as Nate sat up.

'What have I missed?' he asked, yawning.

I blinked: crikey, where to start? But Captain Farley was tapping his watch. There were energy drinks to be made, maps to be read, goose fat to be warmed so it was easier to smear on.

'I've got news – brilliant, bizarre news, in fact,' I whispered to Nate. 'I'll tell you on the way to the boat.'

*

The harbour was a five-minute walk away. I made sure Nate and I were a few paces behind the captain and Mrs Lamb before I told him.

'The captain says he's going to help us swap places.'

Nate gave me a sideways look. 'Are you making this up?'

'No! I'm deadly serious. He knows everything!'

'He's not going to report us to the officials?'

'He didn't say so, no. I think he's on our side.'

Nate blinked in amazement. 'That's extraordinary!'

'It is,' I agreed.

'But then he always thought you were the better choice, didn't he?'

'You don't mind?' I asked, worried that he had been enjoying all the attention.

Nate laughed. 'Cripes almighty, of course not! I'm delighted for you, old chum. If I've helped you as much as you've helped me, then . . .' He trailed off. 'How's it going to work, though?'

'Not sure exactly,' I admitted. 'All he said was for us to follow our plan.'

'Well, the pilot won't be in on it.'

'Nor will the other boat with the film crew!'

So it was still going to be tricky. The pilot, when he realised, might insist on turning back. And the film crew would see absolutely everything. But as long as they didn't interfere . . . All we could do was try.

*

At the harbour, two boats were waiting, engines idling: the larger of the two, lit up like a casino, was for the film crew, Mr Wrigley and Mrs Lamb. Before boarding Mrs Lamb had a final word with Nate.

'I picked the best person for this swim, I truly believe that, so don't let me down.'

I didn't dare look at Captain Farley or Nate.

Our pilot boat was called the *Maybelle*. Before the Channel swimming craze, she'd been used for fishing: she still smelled of it, and was strung with ropes, floats and all manner of hooks and hatches. Once on board, we set off promptly. Every boat had its time slot, and there were other pilots scheduled to make the same trip later that night. It still amazed me that Channel swimming had become so popular.

'It'll be a tad choppy for the first few miles,' Mr Hawkins warned as we chugged out of the harbour. 'But the forecast is decent.'

As soon as we left the protection of the harbour walls, the sea sprang up to meet us. The *Maybelle* tipped and lurched as the wind blew hard into our faces. The boat swung round towards the beach, then slowed for Nate to climb the ladder down into the water. The distance back to the shore was thirty yards, and from here, at the pilot's signal, the swim would officially begin.

I watched, legs twitching, as the final preparations were made. Nate took off his sweater, secured his orange hat. Captain Farley passed him the jar of goose fat, which Nate rubbed on his neck, in his armpits and all the other places that chafed on a long, long swim. His hands were shaking.

So far so good. He was acting the part perfectly. When Mr Hawkins wasn't looking, I pulled on my swimming hat and goggles. I waited for Nate's signal. It was coming. Any moment now.

Captain Farley gave a curt nod. 'Godspeed, Nate.'

Nate, slapping his arms around his torso, went to the edge of the boat. My heart raced as I watched him hesitate.

'Everything all right?' the captain asked.

Nate turned to us. 'Please, sir, I'd like Nellie to start the swim with me.'

I was already scrambling out of my clothes and slapping on goose fat.

'A top idea,' the captain agreed. 'Let's get you both in the water, shall we?'

'Hold on!' Mr Hawkins interjected. 'Surely it'd be best to save Nellie for later, when you're tiring?'

'It's the boy's choice,' the captain replied, then said to us, 'Though remember the rules. No contact once the swim starts. Two hours of swimming together, no more. We'll get you back on board, Nellie, once he's into his stride.'

A look of understanding passed between us: he knew *this* would be the critical moment when the swap would take place. We climbed down the ladder, me first, Nate right behind. Excitement skittered across my skin. Our plan was working.

The short swim took us to Shakespeare Beach. There, we stood at the shoreline, both flexing our feet, shaking out our limbs, ready to enter the water again. Thirty yards out to sea, the *Maybelle*'s lights bobbed above the water. Captain Farley and Mr Hawkins stood at the handrail: two dark shapes hunched together, discussing, no doubt, timings, wind direction and speed. To the right was the film crew's boat, windows lit up, the railings lined with people.

I blocked out the fluttering thrill of what we were about to do. It was time to concentrate and imagine reaching the end. *Picture the French coast*, I told myself. *Imagine Lena's there on the beach, holding your towel, like she used to do at the gravel pits.*

'Ready?' I asked Nate.

He swallowed loudly. 'Ready.'

The *Maybelle*'s engine changed pitch. On board a torch flashed three times, then the little boat's horn honked loudly. It was our signal to begin.

25.
SUMMER, 1952
NELLIE

We walked into the water, a few feet apart. The sea was cold enough to make Nate catch his breath. Up to our left, cheers rained down from the harbour wall where a crowd had gathered. The noise became fainter as we began swimming and left the beach behind. Ahead, on the water, two boats: to the right, still, the film crew, their bright lights sweeping the waves, directly in front the *Maybelle* chugging steadily into the dark. It was the *Maybelle* we focused on. We'd been told not to swim too close to the engine because the diesel fumes would make us sick. So I let Nate take the lead, tucking myself in behind. Captain Farley watched from the boat's railings.

'Pace yourselves,' he reminded us. 'You've only been going five minutes. Settle in and find your rhythm.'

As Nate's stroke lengthened, I concentrated on my own.

Breathe, arm, kick, kick.

Captain Farley's torch stayed fixed on Nate, as the film crew and the pilot would be expecting. I didn't mind the darkness. There were no stars, no moon. The sky was heavy, blackish-blue, and seemed to spill down into the sea. I imagined I was swimming with my eyes closed. We'd been warned there would be waves at first, but the sea had already quietened to a gentle swell.

Up on the boat, Captain Farley moved away from the railings. Someone was brewing coffee. Over the throb of the engine, I heard Mr Hawkins's throaty laugh. I settled into the swim.

Breathe, arm, kick, kick.

*

We might've been swimming ten minutes, or an hour. I was swimming well, in a smooth, steady rhythm, and my mind began to wander on to other things.

'Don't ever be ordinary,' Mam had told me.

But sometimes, I wished I was. I'd have loved to have gone home each night to my own mum and dad, to sit down for supper in the house I'd been born in. Yet if my life had been normal, I'd never have met Lena, or Nate.

I wouldn't be here now, swimming to France.

I kicked on through a cold current, glad when it warmed again. Over to my right, on the film crew's boat, the cameraperson kept following Nate's every move. Ahead, on the *Maybelle*, Captain Farley's beam swung over me before finding Nate's head.

'Your two hours is almost up,' he warned.

I felt good, still: no aches, no pains, and I'd hardly thought about the cold.

It was time to swap.

Nate and I stopped, treading water. The swap itself would be straightforward enough now the captain was in on it. All we needed was to be a safe distance from Mr Hawkins's eagle eyes. The rest we'd trust to our matching costumes and orange hats and pray they made us indistinguishable from each other, as had been the case at the gravel pits.

At this point, Mr Hawkins should've been steering the boat. But instead, to our great frustration, he was leaning against the railings, only a few feet from where we'd changeover. Light from the *Maybelle* and the film crew's boat lit up the sea around us, as well as the ladder and the side of the boat. Mr Hawkins would see everything. When Nate climbed out it would be blindingly obvious it wasn't me.

'What do we do now?' Nate hissed.

I glanced worriedly up at the captain, who understood the situation.

'Shouldn't you be steering, man?' he barked at the pilot.

Mr Hawkins stiffened. 'All right, no need for that tone.'

But he did disappear from view, which made it safe for Captain Farley to beckon Nate to come alongside the boat: Nate, though, didn't move.

'What's the matter?' I asked.

'Something's on my leg!' he yelped.

'What is? What's wrong?'

'Arrggghh! It's biting me!'

My first thought was: shark! Wasn't there a Channel swimmer who'd been bitten by a great white? Hadn't they died? Panic scrambled my brain.

'Stay back, Nellie!' Captain Farley yelled, as I swam closer to try and help.

Mr Hawkins appeared again. 'Do NOT touch him! Remember the rules!'

'But he's being attacked!' I cried.

'Get it off me, Nellie!' Nate screamed.

I didn't know what to do.

'Hey! What's happening? Everything okay?' a film

crew person called from their boat.

Captain Farley pointed at something in the water.

'Could it be a jellyfish?'

'Most likely. They're a common hazard in these parts,' Mr Hawkins confirmed.

I was relieved to hear it: a jellyfish had to be better than a shark, surely. Yet if Nate's yelping and squealing was anything to go by, he was still in a lot of pain. We had another problem now too. Even if we were wearing the same orange hats, the same costumes, the second Nate got out of the water we'd see a sting mark on his foot. Mr Hawkins would tell us apart in an instant. As would the film crew. As would Mrs Lamb and Mr Wrigley.

Nate's groaning turned angry: 'Is someone going to help me here? It's stuck to my leg!'

'Hold on, lad!' Mr Hawkins called.

He disappeared again, reappearing moments later with a broom.

'A broom handle usually does the trick,' Mr Hawkins instructed, passing it to me. 'Flick the beast off with it and you've not touched the lad. Job done.'

I swam alongside Nate.

'Okay, lift your leg,' I told him. 'Up a bit, so I can see it.'

Wincing, he raised his right leg above the water. I was expecting something white, but the jellyfish was an ugly, reddish-brown blob. It was an absolute whopper, the size of a dinner plate, and covered not just his foot but also his shin. I aimed the broom, swinging it hard, but the swell of the sea shifted me too high, and I caught Nate hard on the knee.

'Arrgghh!' he cried. 'You're supposed to be helping!'

The next swing got right under it. The jellyfish lifted like a giant scab, and flew off into the sea.

'What did the jellyfish look like? Did you see it?' the captain wanted to know.

'Big, brown,' I said. 'Hairy-looking underneath.'

The captain repeated what I'd said to Mr Hawkins, who was busy steering the boat. The engine note dropped. The pilot reappeared at the railings, making frantic arm movements to Nate.

'You'll have to come in!' he insisted. 'If it's a lion's mane we need to get the sting out. I'm sorry, but there we are.'

We knew what this meant.

Once Nate was out of the water, in full view of everyone, the swim was over. The *Maybelle* would turn back for Dover.

Even Nate, who was looking weak, hesitated.

'I could try swimming for a bit longer,' he suggested.

'Don't be daft,' I told him.

Two pairs of arms reached down to help Nate up the

ladder. I swam closer, ready to climb on board after him. Any moment the disappointment of giving up was going to hit me like a ship's wave.

A shout from the film crew's boat made everyone look around.

'Hey! We're still filming! Keep him swimming, can't you?' the person yelled.

'He's injured!' the pilot shouted in reply. 'We'll have to take him back to Dover.'

'Whoa! Hang on there! How injured is he?'

'He needs medical attention.'

'Could he not *try* to keep going? Is that possible?' the film person suggested. 'It'd make great footage, guys, and we are trying to make a film here. That's what you signed up for.'

The pilot looked flustered. Once again Captain Farley took charge.

'Don't touch the boat, Nellie!' he ordered. 'Stay exactly where you are!'

I stared at him in surprise. 'Shouldn't I come in?'

He shook his head, then said something to Mr Hawkins in a fast, urgent voice.

'The *girl*?' The pilot frowned at me. 'Won't it be obvious?'

'Not if she keeps her distance from both boats.'

'Is she any good, though?'

'The very best,' Captain Farley replied.

*

For the next while, I swam in a kind of fever dream. Nothing had gone to plan. Yet in the end we'd not had to do much pretending, and here I was, swimming the English Channel. At one point, Captain Farley shouted, 'Feed time!' and a bottle tied to a rope was thrown from the boat, landing with a slap beside me. I took a huge swig: the Ovaltine was cold but tasted sweet and delicious.

A while later, I noticed the sky was changing. There was light up ahead along the horizon, a soft blue glow, and the sea became more than one colour. My heart soared.

Daylight!

As the sun climbed higher it made the water glitter like pennies, and threw my shadow on to the hull of the boat. This was now my swimming partner, our arms rising and falling in perfect togetherness.

'You're halfway!' Captain Farley shouted from the deck.

A little later, from the film crew boat, another shout:

'How's the boy doing? He's swimming real good,' then a loud whistle and a cheer: 'Keep going, Nate!'

They assumed he was the one in the water. Our plan, even now, was still working. It gave me a much-needed boost, because at this point I was beginning to flag.

Sometime later, Nate appeared at the railings, still wearing his costume and orange hat. His foot was covered in a wet cloth.

'They got the sting out!' he hissed, crouching down so the film crew wouldn't see too much of him. 'And I've had coffee and ham sandwiches!'

It was a relief to hear he felt better, but I'd have died for a hot drink and a sandwich. Next feed time, it was more Ovaltine. My mouth was sore from the salt water, and swallowing wasn't so easy. Then we had to swim around a huge oil tanker that appeared in our path. Those extra yards were a struggle. And when the tanker had passed and there was still no sign of France, I began to tire even more. The muscles in my shoulders were burning; my hips ached. This was the longest swim I'd ever done – by *hours* – and I wasn't sure if I could keep going.

Once the doubts started, they quickly overwhelmed me. I struggled to get my stroke right. My arms and legs seemed to be fighting against me. The captain must've seen the change because he threw me another bottle.

'Coffee!' he said.

The drink was warm, bitter, and sent a blast of energy through me. When I'd finished, he threw down a chocolate biscuit. I didn't care that it was wet and salty, and crammed it in my mouth.

'Five miles out!' Mr Hawkins called.

Nate appeared on deck again, pointing excitedly up ahead. 'Nellie, look! You have to see it! There's France!'

Lifting my head from the water, I saw, finally, a dark smudge on the horizon. I'd imagined this moment so often, and yes, the French coastline did look like heaven. Five miles meant a few more hours swimming, but the sight of land made it feel possible again. I could – I would – do this.

My focus now was to get through the next couple of hours. I tried not to think about the pain in my shoulders and hips. Head down, I concentrated on my stroke.

Breathe, arm, kick, kick. Breathe, arm, kick, kick.

As my body settled again, the French coast became ever clearer. I could make out the colours of it now, the pale sand, the mottled rocks, the green sweep of land rising up from the beach. It looked quite a lot like England.

'You're nearly there, old chum,' Nate encouraged me. Then, a bit later, 'I can see people on the beach!'

After that, he went quiet, worried no doubt about how he was going to explain what had happened to his father, and to the film crew. It would be one heck of a shock to everyone when I got out of the water. I tried to concentrate on keeping to my rhythm. But I kept thinking how lucky Nate was, having his family there waiting for him. How I wished that someone would be there for me, to cheer when I walked up the beach. I began to feel upset, and then angry.

Soon every single thing annoyed me – the boat cutting off my view of the coast, Nate and the captain and Mr Hawkins, drinking coffee and eating sandwiches, the film crew playing awful music through loudspeakers, and someone with a megaphone reminding me that I was on course to be the first child to do this, ever.

When Nate tried to talk to me again, I told him to shove off. It brought the captain straight back to the railings.

'Give me a wave!' he said. 'Show me you're all right!'

I tried to ignore him. What a stupid waste of energy! My arms were for swimming, not waving! I wished he'd stop fussing and go away. But he didn't.

'You're only a mile offshore now, but the current's strong so you'll need to be careful. Listen to me, Nellie.'

I tried. But everything in my head was jumbled. I

couldn't think a sensible thought or speak a single word. I knew I had to listen to the captain so I could reach the shore safely, but my anger had dulled to total and utter exhaustion. I didn't care any more. I just wanted to stop. Mrs Lamb had called this part of the swim 'the wall'. Lots of swimmers hit it: the crucial thing was to keep going.

Breathe, arm, kick, kick.

On the headland, I could see a row of white buildings, gleaming against the blue sky. There looked to be a lighthouse up there too.

'You're aiming for that cove.' Now it was the pilot talking and pointing. 'There, to the left of those rocks.'

I lifted my head to hear the sound of waves breaking on sand. The beach was only small, with no obvious way down to it. And yet standing there, just as Nate said, was a group of people. The Clatworthys, I guessed – Mr, Mrs, Nate's younger brother – and more reporters, more cameras ready to capture the story.

'Keep to the left of the boat. It'll shelter you from the crosswind,' the pilot advised.

'You're only five hundred yards out now!' cried the captain.

'That's five lengths of the gravel pits! You can do this!' The third voice was Nate's.

I kept kicking, kept moving my arms in time with my feet, but the voices sounded very far away. I was too tired. The current was pulling at me, driving me on past the beach, and it was so much easier just to give in and go with it. I couldn't fight. All I wanted was for someone to tell me I could stop. I'd done my best, I'd had a go, but it was all right to give up.

It was then I sensed someone moving alongside me in the water. I turned, expecting to see Nate and his bandaged foot, supporting me for the final push. But there was no one there – or rather, if there was, it wasn't a person: it was a shaft of sunlight, turning the murky water bright. Something – someone – was urging me on. My arms began to move more freely, the pain in them easing, and I felt that yes, I could do this, and I'd be all right. Maybe it was just the shelter of the boat, or maybe someone *was* guiding me in. A lucky spirit, maybe, a selkie. Or my mam.

Over the crashing waves came the sound of cheering and yelling. The *Maybelle* slowed and cut its engine. I swam past the boat, past the shouts of the captain, Mr Hawkins, Nate. From behind me different voices:

'This looks brilliant! Get a close-up of him coming out of the water if you can!'

Breathe, arm, kick, kick.

Just a few more strokes and I'd be there. My feet brushed against sand, then shingle. I touched the bottom of the sea, and immediately my legs gave way. I sat down with a splash. Someone from the beach came racing out through the breakwaters towards me.

'Don't touch her!' A voice from the boat. 'She has to walk three steps up the beach!'

I stood up, focusing on the place where the waves were breaking. My legs buckled again. I sank down. Stood up. Sank down. Everything was white and swirling. I crawled on my knees to the water's edge. Slowly, shakily, I got to my feet.

One step.

Two steps.

Three steps . . .

Until a sea of arms went around me.

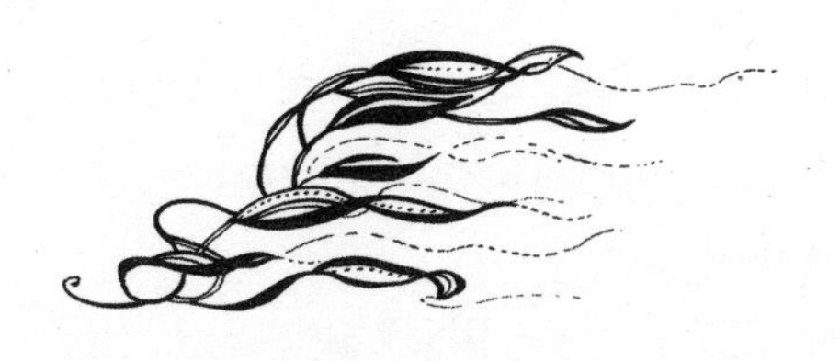

26.
SUMMER, 1952
NELLIE

It was Ma Blackwell who handed me my towel. Her face, stern and soft and so familiar, swam in front of my eyes.

'You silly, clever girl, you!' she cried.

Mr Blackwell was there too, in his best Sunday suit: each taking an arm, they helped me further up the beach.

'What are you doing here?' I gasped. Monday was market day in town, and they always went, so they couldn't be here in France. I had to be dreaming.

'And miss this? Not likely!' Ma Blackwell exclaimed.

Mr Blackwell's voice shook with feeling. 'Our Nellie, the first kiddie to swim all the way to France! Imagine that!'

At this point my legs gave out again. I sank on to the shingle beach and began to sob – proper, exhausted, wrung-out tears. The Blackwells crouched next to me, rubbing my back and handing me hot, sweet tea from a flask.

'You did it!' Mrs Blackwell said. 'My goodness, girl, you did it!'

'So go on, have a good blub. You deserve it,' Mr Blackwell urged.

I smiled. Laughed. Cried even harder, though not just that this wild dream of mine had actually come true. The Blackwells were calling me 'our Nellie', and it felt wonderful to be someone's again. How they knew that I was doing the swim instead of Nate, and how they afforded the ferry, I didn't know, but I suspected Captain Farley was behind it.

'Where is Nate?' I asked then, looking around.

Mr Blackwell nodded towards the water's edge: 'Looks like his father's on the case.'

Mr Clatworthy was standing knee-deep in the sea, calling out to the pilot boat that was moored twenty yards offshore. On the other boat, Mrs Lamb waved her arms about in a very angry fashion. Mr Wrigley was with her, spectacles glinting in the sun. And next to him the bulky black shape of a camera, and a person crouched behind it, still filming.

'Oh heck.' I huddled into my towel.

I'd known this was coming, the moment when everyone realised what we'd done. It was going to be messy and difficult, trying to explain ourselves. Already a full-scale shouting match had broken out down at the shoreline.

'Don't you tell *me* the rules of Channel swimming!' Mrs Lamb was yelling. 'Your son and his little pal have made idiots of all of us! It's a disaster!'

'Where the blazes *is* my son?' Mr Clatworthy shouted back. 'That's what's concerning me, frankly!'

It was worrying me too: where *was* Nate? He'd been up on deck not so very long ago – limping, yes, but seeming to be okay. Had the jellyfish sting got worse? Was he suddenly, badly ill?

Scrambling to my feet, I joined Nate's dad at the sea's edge.

'Mr Clatworthy,' I began. 'Nate had a – oh!'

I stopped, choked with relief, as Nate reappeared on deck.

'What's happened?' Mr Clatworthy cried, noticing Nate's foot, which was wrapped in a comically fat bandage. 'Was there an accident?'

'Yes, with a big brown jellyfish,' I explained. 'They got the sting out, though, so fingers crossed he's all right.'

As if to prove he was, Nate swung his good leg over

the side of the boat. Captain Farley warned him not to jump, that they'd get him to shore, if he could just wait. Poor Mr Hawkins looked utterly exasperated.

'In all my born years, I've never known a swim like this one!' he cried.

Of course, Nate couldn't wait. I watched, heart in mouth, as he heaved his other leg – the bad one – over the railings, and jumped into the sea. He landed neatly enough, called out, 'Bravo, old girl!' to me.

Yet the waves were breaking messily around him. The current, as I knew, was strong, and Nate, weak from the jellyfish sting, was struggling. I felt a jolt of fear: this was not how things were meant to end. Flinging off my towel I ran into the water. As I did so, Mr Clatworthy charged past me, fully clothed, to dive beneath the waves. Moments later, he appeared next to Nate.

'I'm all right, Dad,' Nate spluttered. 'I can manage,' though he clearly couldn't.

Without any fuss, Mr Clatworthy put his arms under Nate and guided him back to the shore. They came in together. When Nate's feet touched down, he stumbled. Before the sea could swamp him, Mr Clatworthy scooped him up and carried him those last few steps up the beach. I gave Nate my towel.

‘What are you doing, jumping in like that?’ I demanded.

He shook the wet hair from his eyes. ‘Had to, didn’t I? To congratulate you. You do realise what you’ve done?’

‘What *we’ve* done,’ I pointed out.

I knew I’d gone beetroot red, but I didn’t care. Even Mr Clatworthy being there didn’t ruin the moment, though he looked different now he was sopping wet and shivering – less sure of himself, somehow.

‘You’d better tell me all about this jellyfish, Nathaniel,’ he said, trying to sound stern.

Nate’s grin faded. ‘Sorry, Dad. I know you must be disappointed that I didn’t do the swim.’

‘*Disappointed?* That’s not the word I’d use.’ He pointed at Nate’s foot. ‘Though I’m hoping the jellyfish came off worse?’

A look flashed over Nate’s face, as if he wasn’t sure if his father was joking. Mr Clatworthy’s serious expression crumpled and suddenly he was smiling. Nate smiled back, relieved and a bit bewildered.

‘I’m proud of you, son, for trying something so difficult,’ Mr Clatworthy admitted, a little catch in his voice.

I wasn’t sure if he meant our swapping places plan, or the swim itself: it didn’t matter. What did was that when Mr Clatworthy pulled Nate into a hug, his son hugged him back. Though they were soon interrupted by Nate's little curly haired brother, charging over and yelling, 'Let me see your bandage!'

And we all laughed.

In the water, meanwhile, Captain Farley lowered himself into a small rowing boat to come to shore. Mrs Lamb was still fuming, insisting everything was a 'disaster'. What I wasn't expecting was for Mr Wrigley to laugh. And it really was such a huge bear of a laugh we heard its full force on the beach.

'It's the complete *opposite* of a disaster!' he insisted. 'These children have turned this swim into a wonderful epic of a story, and we've filmed every last second of it! It's going to be incredible!'

*

Officially, Mr Hawkins told us, the swim was void. The registered swimmer, the name logged by the association, was 'N. Clatworthy', not N. Foster. The news came a little while later in a hotel dining room where Nate and I were tucking into egg and chips.

'We followed *most* of the rules, though, didn't we?' I reasoned.

Nate speared a chip. 'Sorry, Nell. I know how much

this meant to you.'

'*Means*,' I corrected him. 'It's not over. I'm going to relive this day for the rest of my life!'

Besides, I didn't do the swim for glory or for my name to be up on a wall somewhere, or because, like Mrs Lamb and Mr Wrigley said, it'd become the newest craze. I did it because I wanted to. I did it to prove to myself I could keep going when times got tough, and that being stubborn, being a 'sticker at things', was actually a strength. And I did it for my best friend, because without Lena making me believe it was possible – that *anything* was possible – I would've grudgingly accepted Mrs Lamb's decision to choose Nate, and that would've made two of us miserable.

'Wish Lena could've been here, that's my only regret,' I admitted.

And yet Mr Clatworthy's reaction had almost made up for it. He must've come to France hoping his son would make the record books, and instead discovered he'd let a girl from Syndercombe take all the glory. I'd still not got over the hug he'd given Nate.

'Was your dad really okay about it?' I asked.

'Actually, he was.'

'What did he say to you in your hotel room?'

'Well, I told him about you, about how you were

positively *dying* to do the swim and I . . . well, I wasn't, frankly, and how we'd conjured up the plan, so I'd not be sent back to school, and you'd get a stab at your dream – and the sponsorship deal money, to boot.'

'He didn't mind?'

'He didn't. I think it shocked him to see the lengths I'd go to, to *not* go back to school. In fact . . .' Nate paused. 'He actually apologised for not listening when I told him about the bullies. And he said I'd done something he'd failed to do, and that was make friends in Syndercombe.'

'It's hardly the same, though. You don't work for the water board. You didn't stretch the truth.'

'That may be so. But as I've told you before, my father rarely approves of anything I do, so I'm counting this as a small victory.'

Which I took to mean that despite the difficult, complicated relationship he had with his father, this was an unexpected step in the right direction.

We'd barely finished our chips when Captain Farley came striding into the dining hall with Mrs Lamb and Mr Wrigley. There was something in the way that *he* was leading *them* towards our table that made my insides flutter with sudden excitement.

'Hullo, Nellie.' The captain stopped at our table, hands clasped behind his back. He was, I could see, trying to be upright and serious, but struggling not to smile.

'Well . . .' He cleared his throat. 'The officials have agreed that—'

Mrs Lamb interrupted: 'Oh, for goodness' sake, don't prolong the agony!'

'What?' I cried. 'What have they agreed?'

'That you did it, Nellie.' Captain Farley beamed at me. 'They've studied the film crew's footage, and agree you followed the rules. Officially you *are* the first child to swim the Channel.'

I stared at him, open-mouthed.

'Congratulations, my dear!' Now it was Mr Wrigley coming forward, his hand outstretched for me to shake. 'We're awful proud to be your sponsor. This is a great day for Wrigley's.'

I almost laughed: it all felt too unreal. But suddenly Nate was leaning across the table, clapping me on the back, and Mrs Lamb, looking me up and down, said she always knew I had it in me.

'Thank you,' I muttered, in an absolute daze. 'Thank you.'

Needing to tell the Blackwells, I went outside to the terrace where they'd been drinking tea in the afternoon sun.

'T'int nothing like our milk, is it, eh?' Ma Blackwell was

saying as she sipped. 'Creamier – oh, here's our champ!'

I pulled up a chair, grinning from ear to ear. '*Officially* the champ, so I've just heard.'

Ma Blackwell's teacup clattered down in its saucer. She threw her arms around me. 'Oh, Nellie Foster!'

'Ah, but are we still allowed to call you that, now you're famous?' said Mr Blackwell with a twinkly smile.

Untangling myself from the hug, I asked what he meant. Especially as Ma Blackwell was shaking her head and shushing him, and he'd the hangdog look of someone who has just said something they're not meant to.

'What's going on?' I demanded.

'Nothing,' Ma Blackwell insisted.

'Wasn't he going to tell her today?' hissed Mr Blackwell at the exact same moment. 'When he gave her the passport?'

At the sound of approaching footsteps, Ma Blackwell flapped her hand for us to be quiet. Captain Farley, still smiling, and looking very unlike his usual serious self, stepped out on to the terrace.

'Ah, Nellie, might I have a word?' he said, then glanced at the Blackwells. 'In private.'

We moved to a quieter part of the terrace, but not before I heard Mr Blackwell say: 'Told you he'd tell her today.'

I felt nervous all over again, but braver too, somehow.

Whatever the captain was about to say, I knew I could probably face it. The captain sat down to speak: I stayed on my feet. First, he handed me a passport. *My* passport, I realised, proudly.

'You needed certain paperwork to land in France, even as an extra on the pilot boat,' he explained.

'Oh, crikey.' I'd forgotten all about passports. 'Thank you for arranging it.'

He stayed seated, as if he had more to say.

'The paperwork . . . ahem.' He started again. '*On* the paperwork I had to give details of your next of kin – your parents, Nellie.'

I swallowed.

'I do believe you to be of an age now where you are old enough to hear the truth.' He took a deep breath. 'Your mother and I . . . I'm—'

'The person who put the yellow roses on her grave?' I guessed at last.

He looked at me, looked away, nodded.

It all added up. 'And the swimming classes, the poetry book, helping us swap places—'

Now it was Captain Farley's turn to interrupt. 'Yes, you're right. I tried to make sure you had what you needed, Nellie. I couldn't do it officially, not without scandal, but I paid an allowance to your mother every month, and after she died, continued to pay it to the Blackwells, with increases when required.'

'That's why Ma Blackwell was at the hall that day,' I realised, remembering her signature on the paperwork.

'Ah, yes, indeed.'

I should've been shocked: maybe I would be later, when it'd properly sunk in. But I already had a hunch that the captain and my mother had been friendly, I'd just not wanted to admit it. All those times Lena and I had played our stupid Mamas and Papas game, and that one single time she'd mentioned him, it'd felt too close to the mark. I wished she was here now to hear this conversation: she always did have a way of making the difficult things seem easier.

'You're my father, that's what you want to tell me, isn't it?' I asked.

Captain Farley blinked. His nose was red, his eyes filling up, but I didn't want him to cry, at least not until he'd said the words out loud. So I waited until he'd composed himself with another deep, shaky breath.

'Yes,' he said. 'I am your father.'

I let it hang there between us for a moment.

'I'm glad you told me,' I then replied.

And for the first time ever, just to see how it felt, I took his hand.

27.
SUMMER, 1952 AND BEYOND
NELLIE

We caught the boat back to England later that day. Ma Blackwell was insistent that I shouldn't miss any more school. And actually, I soon appreciated the normality of a daily routine. Putting on my uniform, sitting in class, queueing for lunch in the canteen helped keep my feet on the ground when everything else in life had become a giddy whirl.

After school and at weekends, I did interviews and went to photo sessions, answered telephone calls and letters. I shouldn't have worried about the press not liking us: once they heard about the jellyfish sting, and Nate's background as the son of the water board engineer sent here to flood our valley, they were falling over themselves to get our full story. We were on radio shows, in magazines, plastered over the front pages of the national newspapers. It was a funny, dizzying time, and took some getting used to.

To begin with I felt dull and awkward, and let Nate do the talking. But gradually I learned to open up a little. What people wanted to hear about was my life as a Channel swimmer. The trick was learning to play the part. Underneath it all I was still me, still Nellie, the girl who liked horses and currant buns and hated spellings and boring school assemblies. I bet Gertrude Ederle, my hero, probably played her part too.

Around this time I began to fully appreciate all the Blackwells had done for me. They'd seen me through some horribly tough times by giving me a home. So when they asked if I now wanted to live with Captain Farley, I said, if they didn't mind, I'd rather stay on with them. The Blackwells were like family to me: I knew them in a way I didn't yet know the captain.

'Then make yourself useful and fetch that washing in from the line,' was Ma Blackwell's brisk reply.

Later I overheard her admitting I was the daughter she'd never had. And Mr Blackwell saying if only he'd been able to keep Perry for me, but the garden here was too small.

'It'd break me to lose Nellie now,' Ma Blackwell sobbed as her husband comforted her.

'Thank heavens we don't have to,' he replied.

Being with them, and knowing I'd always be, I felt truly warm and content. Yet even now, if Lena asked me to go with her to London, or Brighton, or India, I doubted I'd have said no. In my heart of hearts, I knew that if she walked in tomorrow I'd still drop everything to be with her.

Months went by and I didn't hear a peep from Lena. When I tried contacting her my letters were returned as 'not known at this address'. All I could do was get on with my life, though it was still hard waking up in the morning and not hearing her voice. I didn't think I'd ever completely get over losing her friendship.

By late winter, work on the reservoir entered its final phase. We'd grown used to seeing water in the fields of the lower valley, yet almost overnight it began creeping towards the village. Landmarks disappeared: a gatepost, a bridge, a front step, a classroom, the remains of a house. The chimneys of Hadfield Hall and the St Mary's spire stayed visible the longest. Then, one March morning, they too were gone.

In brighter news, my swimming continued to go from strength to strength. Exciting times lay ahead. The English Channel craze meant people were constantly coming up with new ways to swim it – in relays, fully clothed, going to France *and* back again in one long stint. Yet we decided, Captain Farley and I, to try America next. The training sessions resumed at the gravel pits, and afterwards, on Saturdays, we'd go for buns in town. Nate, who'd started his new senior school, and came home most weekends, would accompany us – often for the training sessions, *always* for the buns. He was a whole lot happier these days.

In the tea shop, one weekend, I brought up the idea of using my middle name, Mary, instead of Nellie. All the professional swimmers I knew had strong-sounding, grown-up names like 'Gertrude' and 'Joyce'. In America having the right name and image would be all important.

'Mary does sound more serious,' Captain Farley agreed.

'Then why not, old bean?' was Nate's response. 'I was a pompous *Nathaniel* till I met you.'

I laughed: *Nate* definitely suited him better.

*

Back at home, I asked Ma Blackwell what she thought of the idea.

Her eyebrows bristled. 'What silliness! Your name is Nellie!'

'It's also Mary,' I reminded her. 'I'm only swapping

the order round. Anyway, Captain Farley says it's more professional sounding.'

'Does he now?' she said in a rather pointed way.

Sometimes I felt as if I was the only one who didn't know the full story of my mother and the captain.

'Was he really smitten with Mam?' I asked. 'I wish you'd tell me about it.'

Ma Blackwell patted a place next to her on the settee.

'I suppose you're old enough to hear,' she agreed. 'They was good friends for years – loved poetry and books, they did – and when your mother couldn't get to the local library, she'd borrow books from the hall.

'Things got . . .' She hesitated, '. . . *complicated* when the war broke out. Your mam was going to have a baby and the captain wanted to marry her and be a family, but your mam, well, some say she didn't love him enough. Others say she'd already given her heart to a soldier, and was waiting for him.'

'The plastic ring,' I murmured. 'Maybe it was true.'

'What I can say is your mam had her own way of doing things.'

'She was stubborn, like me, d'you mean?'

Ma Blackwell smiled. 'Something like that, yes.'

*

And so, Nellie Foster, shy, mouse-haired schoolgirl, grew into Mary Foster, the world-famous swimmer. The following year, I went to America and swam the Catalina Channel, which was another adventure entirely. Often stories about me made the newspapers. But equally often there'd be bigger news, like the coronation of our new queen and how, on the very same day, Edmund Hillary climbed Everest – the real Everest, not the swimmer's version.

It was after returning home from abroad one time that I saw a letter for me on the hall table. I knew the writing straight away. So did my heart, which gave a painful double kick. Dropping my suitcases, I fumbled open the envelope. I should've waited till I'd taken off my coat and was sitting down, but I had to read it immediately.

'Dearest Nell,' it began.

'By the time you read this you'll be world famous, and will barely remember me (you'd better do, though!), I've read all about you in the newspapers – every single article, and yes, I cut them out, though not to pin on my bedroom wall. I keep them in my special 'Nellie Foster' scrapbook and it's filling up fast! You've done so amazingly, brilliantly well – swimming the English

Channel, the Catalina Channel – where next?! The Olympics?

I'm coming to the part that I have to write. I owe this to you, Nell, and I'm sorry it's taken me so long to give you the explanation you deserve. I wish life was simpler, and by that I mean families in particular. I always thought wild horses wouldn't drag me away from you, and then, that day at the station, they did.

You'll remember my baapu was working hard to set up a business, and to pay for my mata to join us from India? You might also remember how, in those last months at Combe Grange, the payments he was sending me were less than usual. Well, he was trying to buy Mata a ticket to England, that was why. I had no idea she was coming, Nell. They didn't tell me in case the plan changed.

Of course, it was incredible to see my whole family. But it was also sad being in London again, with all the bomb sites and people saying Indians didn't belong here, when the government had *invited* us to come. I missed you too – and Nate, and the Blackwells, and Perry and Sage. Our life in the village felt so pure compared to the big, smelly city. And part of me knew that if I wrote to you, and you wrote back, I'd come running, and Baapu's dream of our family reunited would be ruined. I suppose the village has gone now, anyway. But I'll never forget our time there.

As it turned out, none of my family liked London. And as the damp, dirty air made my chest bad again, we decided to move somewhere warm, somewhere that welcomed us, and felt like home.

When you read this I'll be in India, back in the Punjab. I don't think I'll ever fit in somewhere the way I do here, Nellie. I loved living with you in Syndercombe, but sooner or later, I knew I'd have to come home. The swimming, the Blackwells, Captain Farley – all that was *your* life. There came a point when *I* had to think about what I wanted. Here, I'm not on the outside of life, or waiting to be sent somewhere else. I'm a Punjabi. This is where I belong.

I hope you understand even just a little bit of what I'm saying. And I hope you find a place to belong too, although I think swimming gives you that already. I'm always with you – in your thoughts, in your dreams – and one day, even if we're too old to speak or laugh, we *will* be together again, I know it in my bones.

Until then, Nellie Foster, Champion Channel Swimmer, please stay brilliant,

Your dearest friend,

Lena.'

As soon as I'd finished reading it, I started from the top again. I kept reading until my tired brain understood what she was telling me. Lena had always been far more than my lucky mascot: she loved me yes, but she also had her own life to live.

Later, in the quiet of my bedroom, I'd cry my heart out for all we'd planned to do together, and how we'd promised to go through life side by side. Yet once Ma Blackwell had made me a cup of tea and sliced me some fruit cake, I felt more hopeful. I was glad for Lena, glad she still considered herself my dearest friend. One day, somehow, we *would* be together again: I hoped she was right about that.

28.
SUMMER, 2032
POLLY

I've been on the edge of my seat the whole time, listening.

'Did you see Lena again?' I have to ask Mary.

'No.'

'Oh!' I'm surprised. Disappointed. 'Why not?'

'Because—' Mary falters as if she's not sure, either. 'Because I was travelling so much, I suppose. Lena was in India, I was all over the world. We did write for a while, but . . .' She trails off.

I think about Sasha, and how we've lost touch too.

'I guess some friendships don't last for ever,' I say.

'Nonsense!' Mary replies sharply. 'We're still the best of friends. It's not about writing letters or remembering birthdays or that sort of thing, it's about what you feel inside.'

'But wouldn't you like to see her again?'

'*Like* to?' Mary's face lights up. 'If I knew exactly where she was, I'd still drop everything—'

'To be with her,' I finish.

There's a long, thoughtful pause.

'You know, it's cleared my mind, talking to you,' Mary says.

Good, I think, because I still want to hear more.

'What about Nate?' I ask. 'What happened to him?'

'Ah, dear old Nate.' Mary sighs wistfully. 'He was such a clever lad. You know he went to university?'

'Did you marry him?'

'*Marry* him?' Mary looks horrified, then howls with laughter. 'I'm sorry . . . but that's the funniest idea.'

'You were good friends, though,' I point out.

'We were,' she says, still giggling. 'But come on, Polly. You're the modern one. You know us girls don't need a man to be happy.'

Fair.

'Who did he marry?'

'Well.' She takes a hanky from her sleeve to dab her eyes. 'First he became my manager when Captain Far – my *father* – got too old to travel with me. It was Maudie Jennings from the village who caught Nate's eye in the end. *She* became Mrs Clatworthy.'

'Wow!'

Mary chuckles. 'He always did like strong-minded women, that one.'

'Is he still—'

'Alive? No, he died a few years ago,' she says sadly, but still smiling. 'He had a big family with Maudie. A happy life. He deserved it – he was a lovely soul.'

I'm still taking in all Mary's told me, how these three friends stayed loyal to each other pretty much all their lives. I can't quite imagine the same for Sasha and me, somehow.

There's more to Mary's story, even now, I'm sure of it. This isn't the end. But the talking's worn her out. She's fallen asleep in her chair, mouth open, the door handle closed in her lap. The clock on the mantelpiece says it's lunchtime, though it's as dark as evening outside. I've been here ages: time hasn't stood still, and I'll be in trouble if I don't get back to Jessie's.

*

Dad has already arrived to drive us home. Just before we climb into the van and Jessie waves us off, I insist on saying \goodbye to the lake. The outlines of the houses are still visible. Further down the valley what's left of the reservoir lies grey and still. Soon, when it rains, the valley will start to fill up, and everything will be hidden again.

'Funny old holiday, wasn't it?' Joel says, joining me. 'Full of secrets.'

'Like you running away, d'you mean?'

He stiffens slightly. 'I meant, like my dancing, like Mum having a baby, like Sasha posting that clip online. We didn't know any of it before we came here, yet it all came out in the end.'

'Talk to Mum and Dad about school,' I urge him. If Nate and Mr Clatworthy could patch up their differences eventually, then I'm pretty optimistic about our parents listening to Joel. '*Please?*'

'I'll try,' he promises.

I stare out at the lake bed. There are secrets everywhere, aren't there, not just from people we know but the world we live in. Often we're told an idea is progress, that everyone will benefit from it because it's modern and for the future. That's what happened in Syndercombe.

What we're not told is that everything comes at a price. Joel, me, the new baby when she arrives, we're living in the future that Syndercombe gave up its valley for, and I wonder, is it progress when millions more people around the world have since lost their homes to flooding? Who pays them compensation? Who finds them new places to live?

This isn't just Nellie's story: it's everyone's.

*

We make it home to Brighton as the first fat drops of rain start speckling the pavements. On the seafront, the ice-cream shacks are closed, the hotels with the biggest windows have boarded them up against the storm. Out over the sea the sky is a livid orangey blue. The air's so thick you can almost taste the thunder.

'There you all are!' Mum's on the doorstep, looking very definitely pregnant. She laughs when she catches me staring at her bump.

'It's such a relief not to have to hold it in,' she admits.

After Jessie's, our flat feels small and cluttered, but a few days away has made me glad to be home. Mum's made veggie pizzas which we eat on the sofa as rain streams down the window. She tells us more about our baby sister, who's coming in time for Christmas, and it'll be Mum who goes back to work afterwards, running the garden business: Dad will look after the baby.

'It suits us that way,' Mum says.

I think of Nellie's mum, on her own with a baby, and

choosing to be. It must've been tough.

'Was it unusual for people to be single parents like eighty-odd years ago?' I ask.

Joel laughs. 'Random as ever, Pol!'

'Why are you asking?' says Mum, interested.

'Oh, you know . . .' I can't explain the door handle, the late-night swims, so I plump for the homework task I've still not done. 'It's a thing for school.'

Joel pales as I mention it.

'I think getting married was the normal, respectable thing to do,' Mum answers. 'You had the wedding first, then the honeymoon, *then* you moved in together.'

'And if you had a baby on your own?'

'Then you were a strong woman,' Mum says, with admiration. 'You were way ahead of your time.'

I wish Mary could hear this: she'd be proud of her mam.

*

That evening, the storm worsens. The thunder's so loud it hurts my ears and the rain, harder than gravel against the windows, makes the gutters gurgle and drains overflow. Outside, our street looks like a river, and the seafront isn't a road any more but an extension of the beach.

Just before bedtime, the electric goes out and with it the internet, and our phone signal. Downstairs, our neighbour Miss Gee's kitchen is underwater. By midnight, she's up with us, on our sofa, drinking tea and telling Dad all about some super-cool sports car she used to own when she was younger and lived in India. She's got the longest white hair I've ever seen.

'What brought you to Brighton?' Dad asks.

'Ah, the sea air – for my lungs, you see: I had TB in childhood.' She pauses to rub her eye. 'I've family here as well, who've always wanted me to visit, and I've always wanted to come. You could say I've a special attachment to the place.'

I can't help thinking Miss Gee's life story sounds an awful lot like Lena's. Sure, the chances of our neighbour actually being Nellie's friend are ridiculously small, but this summer has been so weird in all sorts of ways.

Is it possible she's Lena?

I doubt it, but the thought doesn't entirely go away.

*

By morning, the worst of the storm is over. It's still raining, though, and there's no electricity. Dad gets out his wind-up radio, and we listen to the news of flooded roads and rail lines, power cuts, damaged houses, and how the emergency services are coping. Miss Gee asks if we can fetch her pills and some clean clothes from downstairs.

'I'll go,' I offer.

Miss Gee's basement flat has its own entrance on the street. It's as I step out on to the pavement that I bump straight into Sasha.

We both start gabbling at once.

'Hi, Pol, I tried to—'

'What are you doing?'

I stop. 'You go first.'

'Um, okay.' Sasha stuffs her hands in her pockets, which makes her shoulders hunch. She's nervous. But I'm not going to make her feel better, not after what she's done to Joel and me.

'I came to say sorry,' she says, staring at her feet, then up at the sky.

For once, I don't say anything.

'The thing is, it wasn't me,' she says. 'That account—'

'Sasha_Torte20?' I interrupt.

She goes red. 'Yup, that one. I know you won't believe me, but my sister set it up, not me. It was her who posted the clip of Joel. Megan filmed it too.'

'In your name?'

'My account's SashaTorte20, remember? No gap or

underscore. Megan posted the clip, then freaked when she saw how much attention it was getting and changed her username. She made it look like I'd done it, but it wasn't me, I promise.'

Sasha's in tears.

I'm confused. If what she's telling me is true, then Megan has done something horrible – not just to Joel and me, but to her own sister.

'Why post the clip in the first place? What's Joel to her?' I ask. My brother's a bit 'out there', always has been, though it's only recently he's been bullied like this.

'Dancing.'

I look at her. Then glance past her as our front door opens. Joel slips out, head down, bag over his shoulder. Something thuds in my chest. He's running away: despite everything we've said, everything we've shared, he's still going to go.

'Hey! Joel!' I cry out.

He freezes. There's a split second where I think he might run for it, but instead, slowly, stiffly, he turns to face me.

'You!' His gaze goes straight to Sasha.

'Where are you going, Joel?' I ask.

He ignores me, still staring at Sasha. 'Who asked you round?'

Sasha reddens. 'I came to see Pol – and you – to—'

'It was Megan,' I interrupt. 'She set up a copycat account.'

'*Megan?* Your sister?' Joel rubs his head, laughs bitterly. 'Yeah, I did wonder. Because of the dance teacher choosing me for the scholarship, not her, right?'

'Right.' Sasha nods, then says to me, 'Your brother and my sister were both up for a scholarship to dance school.'

'The place in London?' I ask Joel.

He nods.

'You said you'd applied,' I remind him. 'You didn't say you'd actually *got* the scholarship.'

'Because I didn't know whether to take it or not. Honestly, Pol, I got so much grief for it at school. It would've been easier just to disappear to London and pay my own way.'

I glance at Sasha, who seems to confirm it.

'Megan was massively upset about not getting the scholarship. She's so competitive – honestly, it's scary, sometimes. That's how everything kicked off.'

Now we know. Joel's been bullied for months and Megan was behind it. It's a shock and a relief. Joel leans against the basement railings, still trying to take it all in.

'Why's it taken all summer for you to tell me?' I ask Sasha.

'Because.' She takes a slow breath. 'When Mum and Dad found out what Megan had done – they heard us fighting about it – they shut down our social media accounts. Well, all but one. They grounded us both.'

'For the whole holidays?'

Her chin crumples slightly, a sign she's upset. 'My mum and dad haven't been getting on for ages, and all this . . . umm . . . well, I think they're splitting up.'

I'm shocked: it's the first time she's ever mentioned her parents not being happy. 'Gosh, I'm sorry, Sash.'

'It's only today that I've been allowed out. I came straight over, through floods and everything.' She holds up a foot to show me her soggy trainers and the wet hem on her jeans. 'I couldn't wait to get out, to be honest – and I wanted to apologise for—'

'Laughing at me swimming? Calling me a poodle?'

She goes red all over again. Hides her face in her hands. 'Arrrgghh, I'm horrible, aren't I?'

'You are. But you're also my friend, and it sounds as if you've had tough summer too.'

'It's not been the best. I've missed you.'

'Me too. And for the record, I've been practising my swimming. Not that I'm suddenly super talented or anything, but I'm getting better.'

Joel looks up at the sky: he's smiling.

'Can we talk about this inside?' he says.

It's raining again, and the smell is fresh and clean and wonderful.

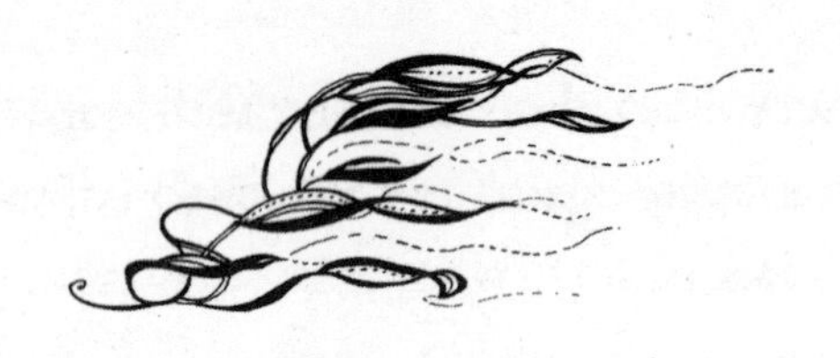

29.
LATE SUMMER, 2032
POLLY

Once I've collected Miss Gee's things, we go back to ours. I'm assuming Joel's in his room because the door's closed. This time, I hope he's unpacked his bag for good. Miss Gee's in the kitchen with us, pretending not to listen in on our conversation.

'Megan should've just accepted it,' Sasha admits to me. 'She didn't get chosen. End of.'

Miss Gee lowers her book. 'What is this about *choosing*?'

I tell her briefly what's happened.

'Huh!' She rolls her eyes dramatically. 'I had a friend who didn't get chosen for something she should've been picked for. We didn't get all shirty about it.'

'What *did* you do?' Sasha asks.

'My dear, we took action to put it right.'

Across the hallway, I notice the door to the sitting room is open. The curtains are closed, and the only light is from a small reading lamp. It takes me a second to realise Joel is in the room. All I can hear is his breathing. He's wearing his headphones, and dancing. I get up from the kitchen, creeping closer for a better look. Sasha follows.

'Wow, he's good, isn't he?' she gasps.

He is. He really, truly is. I've never seen my brother dance like this. This swaying and swirling, as if he's not a human at all, but is made of something else entirely, like mist or smoke. I move into the doorway, leaning against the jamb. I can't take my eyes off him. He twists, spins, reaches his arms up to the ceiling. There's no denying it – he's incredible. Of course he should go to dance school. But properly, sensibly, with the scholarship and our parents' blessing. He doesn't have to run away.

Miss Gee joins us in the doorway.

'So *that's* what's been making all the noise up here,' she says. 'Sounds like a Clydesdale when you're in my kitchen.'

'A *what*?' Sasha's confused.

Perry and Sage, I want to say – they were Clydesdales. I'm surprised Miss Gee knows about working horses: it's not what you'd call common knowledge.

Or maybe I should've trusted my hunch last night. Maybe I'm not surprised at all. I'm pretty sure she's said enough already – about weak chests and India, Brighton and Clydesdales, and not being chosen for things. Still, I'm suddenly nervous.

'What does the G in your surname stand for?' I ask her. 'Is your name Lena, by any chance? Lena Gill?'

Miss Gee's eyes go very wide. 'Who wants to know?'

'Nellie Foster,' I say.

I'm standing so close I hear the breath catch in her throat.

'Nellie? What, *my* Nellie?' she whispers.

And she does something I've not seen Miss Gee do, at least not with me.

She smiles.

*

This, I think, is the ending I've been hoping for: secrets revealed, friendships restored, and the heatwave finally broken. Now all we have to do is put Mary and Lena in touch. Neither has the internet, so it takes longer than you'd think. Everything goes via Jessie, who's still trying to persuade Mary she needs extra support at home. Because of her flooded kitchen, meanwhile,

Lena has moved to a care home further along the seafront. I'm dying for them to video-call each other or talk online, but when Jessie's email eventually arrives, she's taken it one step further. Mary has agreed to come to Brighton, she tells us, to see a lovely sounding care home on the seafront. It also just so happens that Lena is already there.

*

The care home is called Channel View. As it's a weekend I go with Jessie and Mary to see the available room. Lena is expecting us: we told her last night. It's only Mary who's not fully in the picture. If it was up to me I'd have told her too, but Jessie insists that this way's best, and she's the nurse.

Inside, the care home smells like the dining hall at school, though it's far quieter. I'm half expecting Lena to be waiting for us in reception: instead we're met by a young man, lanyard around his neck, who introduces himself as Sunny.

'You must be Miss Foster,' he says to Mary.

Jessie beams at the man. 'She is, yes, hello.'

'I *can* talk,' Mary tells her, and shuffles closer to Sunny so she can shake his hand.

'They think I'm daft, but I'm as sharp as a tack,' she informs him.

He laughs. 'I can tell.'

Sunny suggests taking off our coats and having a cup of tea in the sun lounge, which, he says, opens directly on to the beach.

'This is amazing!' I gasp as we walk in. The room is huge and light, and though there are handrails, a ramp, buttons to press for help, the bright cushions, the driftwood art on the walls make it feel cosy.

Then there's the view.

The glass doors slide back to an area of decking, and beyond that is the shingle, which drops down to the sea. Even with the doors shut you can hear the shushing of the waves, the pebbles rattling.

'Lovely, isn't it?' Jessie whispers to me. 'Though it won't be here in twenty years' time, not with sea levels rising.'

'Nor will I be,' says Mary, who hears.

As Sunny goes off in search of tea, there's still no sign of Lena. I'm getting anxious. Has anyone told her we're here?

We wait. I fidget in my seat. Jessie chats to Mary about the view. When the door to the lounge swings open, I jump. But it's only Sunny with a tea tray and biscuits, which he leaves with us before slipping out. Jessie gives me a reassuring look.

When he returns again, this time Lena is with him. She's wearing a lovely paisley shawl and a pair of green velvet slippers. Mary's still gazing out at the sea.

'Mary?' I tap her gently on the arm. She looks first at me, at the teapot, then up at Lena.

For the longest, tensest moment no one moves.

Then Mary gets up without her sticks. One slow step at a time, she makes her way across the carpet to Lena. There's a look on her face – determined, joyful – that makes me think suddenly of what it felt like to see the coast of France after all that time at sea.

There are tears streaming down Lena's cheeks and dripping off her chin on to her shawl.

'What's the story, morning glory?' Lena asks, her voice cracking.

Mary doesn't miss a beat. 'What's your tale, nightingale?'

Neither woman moves: they're too busy staring at each other.

'I've waited a long time to hear you say that again,' Lena says. 'What kept you?'

Mary shakes her head. 'Always bossy.'

'Always stubborn,' Lena retorts.

Worried this isn't going to plan, I glance at Jessie. But she's smiling. As is Sunny. They've both got tears in their eyes.

'I take it you still want to see the room, Miss Foster?' Sunny asks.

'Nellie,' she corrects him. 'Call me Nellie.'

Lena rushes towards her then, closing the last bit of distance between them. They both start laughing, then crying, then laughing again. They hold each other so tightly their knuckles go white. This, I think, my heart swelling, is their proper ending, though to call it that doesn't feel right, either, when really it's another beginning.

30.
2032 AND BEYOND
POLLY

The following week Nellie moves into Channel View, in a room next door to Lena's. It's interesting to see what she's brought with her from the cottage: on a shelf I spot the Christina Rossetti poetry book, a brass door handle, and something I'd not seen before – a yellow plastic ring. There's also an old leather armchair that, Nellie says, was the one her mother used to sit in to read at Hadfield Hall, and was left by Captain Farley in his will. He left her an awful lot more too – everything, in fact – though it's Jessie who tells me this. Apparently, Nellie gave a big chunk of the money to a sanctuary for Clydesdale horses, and the rest went to an environmental charity for flood victims.

Despite having her own lovely room, Nellie sleeps in

with Lena every night. It's like it used to be all those years ago at Combe Grange. And every morning, catchphrase at the ready, the first thing they hear is each other.

*

Meanwhile, in my world, our baby sister arrives. She's born on a cold day in January, officially ten days overdue. Her name is Rowan, like the tree. We're thrilled to bits to meet her at last, all three and a half red, angry kilos of her, and try not to be offended that she doesn't seem to feel the same about us. She's a very 'screamy' baby. Yet the thing she loves more than anything is dancing with Joel. The second the music comes on and my brother picks her up, Rowan grins and dribbles and bobs along to the beat.

Just before Easter, my brilliant brother is accepted, on his scholarship, to the dance school in London. This time he's done it with Mum and Dad's approval, references from teachers, forms filled in. It means he'll have to stay in London during the week. I'll miss him, of course, but he's promised to come back at weekends. And I'm okay with that because he's happy. Plus, I've got a sister now, so it's not like I've been deserted.

'Look at this, Pol.' One afternoon when he's packing his stuff, Joel shows me a 'Congratulations' card that's signed: 'You deserve this, Megan'.

'That's good, isn't it? It sounds like an apology, really.'

'Yeah,' Joel agrees. 'It does.'

*

When summer comes round again, this year Jessie visits us. It's another hot one: the flat is stifling, noisy, cramped, and I overhear a conversation about Nellie's empty cottage.

'She wants someone living there, keeping an eye on it,' Jessie says to Mum. 'It's got a decent garden for growing your own veggies.'

'We'll think about it,' Mum replies.

But she's smiling more and is definitely worrying less, and Dad's been browsing the tomato pages in his seed catalogue again. I like the idea of moving to the countryside. Though it would mean leaving Sasha, and Nellie and Lena, I'd be going somewhere I feel I've known for years.

The next morning, I catch Jessie out on our balcony, Rowan grizzling on her hip.

'Hey, I'm your auntie so listen to me, okay?' she coos.

Amazingly, Rowan goes quiet and takes a fistful of Jessie's super-long hair.

'Follow your dreams, by all means, baby girl, but don't forget you're not the only human on this planet wanting bigger and better, yeah?'

Rowan gurgles.

Jessie kisses the top of her head. 'Tread lightly, that's all.'

It's sound advice. She's my favourite auntie for a very good reason.

*

Later that day when the temperature drops a little, we go to the beach for a family picnic. I've decided to wear my costume under my clothes. Everyone's covered in sun cream and wearing floppy hats. Nellie and Lena are sitting in the shade under a parasol. Joel, me and Sasha are taking it in turns to help Rowan build sandcastles. The grown-ups are discussing how we'd originally thought Lena's surname was Gee.

'Names are funny things,' Lena agrees.

I catch myself thinking about the reservoir.

'Why did the water board call it *Truth*water Lake?' I ask.

'It wasn't the water board's idea,' replies Nellie.

'Really?'

'Wasn't it?' Like me, Lena is confused.

'No,' Nellie says, firmly. 'The villagers decided it – the Blackwells, Captain Farley, Mrs Lee, Miss Setherton and everyone. The water board wanted to call it Clatworthy Lake, but we protested. It was amazing, really: after all we'd been through, all the lies and the cheating us out of our homes and proper compensation, we put up a real fight, and the water board backed down.'

'So the *truth* bit of the name—?' I ask.

Nellie glances at Lena. 'Is a reminder not to hide things, I suppose. To live an honest life.'

I'm suddenly reminded of that old homework task from last summer.

'What would you say you're most proud of in your life?' I ask them both.

'Oh, Lena,' says Nellie without hesitating. 'Definitely. Without a doubt.'

'Likewise, Nell,' Lena replies.

Dad looks sheepish. 'Cripes, I said tomatoes when you asked me!'

I laugh.

'What about regrets?' I ask Lena first.

She screws up her nose. 'Probably how I rushed off at the station that day when I left Nellie to go home.'

I turn to Nellie.

'No regrets, although I wish I could've kept Perry.' She notices my reaction. 'What? Are you surprised? Did you think I'd say losing Syndercombe or my mother?'

I consider it.

'No,' I decide. 'It makes sense.'

After all the things they've done with their lives – all the travel, the fame, the achievements – the one sure thing for both is each other – and a Clydesdale horse. It makes me think of what Jessie said to Rowan on the balcony earlier, that we all have dreams and it's okay to follow them, but to tread lightly in the world.

I've worried far too much about not being good at anything, about being laughed at, and not having a talent like Joel or Nellie. Yet Dad's tomatoes don't seem such a silly answer any more, because for people who've lived a lot, it's the everyday things that mean the most. We don't have to leave our mark on the world: in fact, wouldn't it be kinder to the planet not to?

And, if that doesn't feel quite satisfying enough for an ending, let's not forget what happened to me last summer. There aren't many people who can say they've time-travelled to the past. Or maybe they've just kept it to themselves: I didn't tell anyone – well, only you.

Nellie holds out her hand. 'Get me up, Polly.'

I help her to her feet, and she starts unbuttoning her dress.

Lena laughs. 'You really did put your costume on underneath, didn't you?'

'Old habits die hard,' Nellie answers.

Following her lead, I take my dress off too. The urge to swim, like that first night at Jessie's, is sudden and overwhelming. Nellie and I stand there, in our costumes, clutching each other's hands.

'Ready?' she asks me.

'Ready,' I reply.

We walk a trail of footprints into the sea. And when the tide comes in and washes them away, it's as if we've never been here, on the beach, but were born in the water, already swimming.

'The Queen of Historical Fiction at her finest.'

Guardian

BRITAIN, OCTOBER 1962

Nothing ever happens in World's End Close. But on the news the Americans and Russians are arguing over missiles in Cuba.

When Stevie discovers a runaway girl in her coal shed, the first thing she does is fetch her best friend, Ray. Both are dying for a bit of adventure, and when the girl begs for help, they readily agree. Yet they soon realise they've taken on more than they bargained for . . .